Survival

Kodie Goldsworthy

 FriesenPress

Suite 300 - 990 Fort St
Victoria, BC, V8V 3K2
Canada

www.friesenpress.com

Copyright © 2018 by Kodie Goldsworthy
First Edition — 2018

Illustrator: Tricia Pathy

ISBN
978-1-5255-2018-1 (Hardcover)
978-1-5255-2019-8 (Paperback)
978-1-5255-2020-4 (eBook)

1. FICTION, SCIENCE FICTION, APOCALYPTIC & POST-APOCALYPTIC

Distributed to the trade by The Ingram Book Company

This book is dedicated to my dad, Jeffery Goldsworthy, who has always been my inspiration in life, for his undying support during this stage in my life. He instilled the desire to become an author when I was a young boy. He was my biggest and only fan, reading everything I wrote, even the five-page comics *That Doctor Robot* and *The Dirty Sink*. I miss him daily; it was always one of his dreams for me to get published. Thank you all who have purchased this book. I truly hope you enjoy reading it as much as I enjoyed writing it. You have made me happy, but more importantly, you have made one of his dreams come true. Rest in Peace, Dad. November 18th, 2016.

TABLE OF CONTENTS

PROLOGUE

It was the year 2023. The earth was a disaster. Society no longer was the rule-maker of life and norms. The only society left was that of those who wanted to survive.

The infection took the world by surprise and spread like a wildfire. Scientists could never pin down where the infection had originated. Religious members preached that it was the work of the Devil for our sins. The first to perish were the Third World countries that couldn't fight the infected with an organized and effective infrastructure. Their militaries were too small to fight a bloodthirsty army of the undead. Once the infection spread from central Africa, through Egypt to the Middle East, the world became one huge battlefield.

Militaries shut down borders. Governments convened, and options were hastily tabled, but there was not enough time to complete them. Society as we knew it failed and fell to the chaos of people in the streets. Animal instincts re-emerged. People killed. People reverted to savagery in order to save themselves.

***

Now the year is 2024. The only countries that have stayed strong and organized are China, Russia, the United States of America, and Canada. They are safe havens for survivors seeking sanctuary from the outside.

The United States of America and Canada have come together as two nations to help each other during this time of chaos and disaster.

China still stays independent, refusing to allow any survivors in and shutting everyone else out for the greater good of China.

Russia has continued to build up its walls and the security of its territory, training young men at the age of fifteen to carry a rifle and help defend the *rodina*, the motherland.

The world population of living humans has plummeted, and resources are scarcer than ever. Life on Earth is different now—the rules are different. The governments have tried to keep society as organized as possible, but the only democratic governments left are Canada and America. China is still governed by the Central Politburo and Russia . . . but no one knows what they have done.

1. HELL

The sun broke through the blinds and lit the room with a golden glow. The sun used to be a nice thing to wake up to—but now it was a sign of just another day in hell.

Black rose from his bed, sitting on the edge, rubbing his eyes. Like all soldiers, scars and bruises covered his body. The stocky Canadian had started his military service in the trenches. Originally a simple grunt, he discovered, through training and practice, that he was a marksman in the rough. Now, at thirty-seven years, he was an accomplished sniper with years of experience and more than enough kills to keep him up at night.

When the infection hit, Sergeant Major John Black was on a recon mission in the Middle East, but he was called back to Canada to help contain the spread. When he arrived home, he was devastated.

Black rose to his feet, made his way to the bathroom and began his day with a shower. A new smell drifted on the gusts of wind that passed through cities and countries worldwide: the smell of death and fear. It ran through the noses and senses of every human across the world, reminding them of the hell that had come upon them. Black got out of the shower and dried off with his towel. Drying his short brown hair, he heard his radio squawk to life.

"Sergeant Major Black, do you copy?" A man's voice in a sea of static. "We got resource duty today."

Black walked over to the radio and picked it up.

"Copy that," he said. "Be there in fifteen."

He tossed his radio onto his bed. Sergeant Major Black and his company were assigned to 19 Wing Comox Air Base to assist in gathering resources every month. Sergeant Major Black put on his tactical pants and long Kevlar shirt, followed by his bulletproof vest and utility belt. Hooking his holsters to both hips, he grabbed his two Browning 9 mm handguns, slid them into the holsters, and buttoned them in. Sliding his boots on and tying them tight, he wrapped his tactical knife around the top of his left boot. Lastly, he collapsed the tripod and slung his sniper rifle over his shoulder.

Black took a deep breath and looked in the mirror. Staring into his reflection, he thought of his wife and daughter, who were savagely taken from him. He thought about how damned much he missed them, and how it wasn't getting any easier.

What the hell do I have left?

After a long moment, Sergeant Major Black opened the door and walked toward the runway.

***

"About time!" said Smith, holding his hands in the air. "That was thirteen minutes and twenty seconds!"

Sergeant Brock Smith was a long-time friend of Black. At thirty years old, he was still the muscle of the team. He kept his head shaved and buffed, sported a black goatee, and had (what seemed to Black) almost unnaturally white teeth. Sergeant Smith's broad shoulders gave him the appearance of raw power and the ability of physical domination. Though Smith had been through hell and back in his military career, he still looked like a pretty boy after missions. Sergeant Smith was second in command after Sergeant Major

Black, but he had never forgotten how he always won their arm wrestle competitions.

"You can't complain," Black said as he walked up the ramp with Smith and got a seat in the heavy transport. Master Corporal Santos, already strapped in, gave Black and Smith a nod.

"Good morning, sir," said Master Corporal Santos.

Sergeant Major Black, as per usual, did not smile or return the greeting.

"Good morning, Master Corporal," said Smith.

Santos nodded to the sergeant and lay back in his seat with his eyes closed.

Master Corporal Andrew Santos was thirty-one. He stood around five foot seven and clocked in at 185 pounds—a well-built man with black spiked hair. He had brown eyes and a scar on his forearm in the shape of a pitchfork from a mission he did way back in the day. He was a quiet man outside the military—mostly a family man who wanted only to go back home at the end of the day and hug his wife and two children. Born in Montréal of first-generation Filipino parents, he had been fighting with the military for ten years.

Corporal Malroy came running up the ramp. "I'm coming!" he yelled as he got to his seat, almost out of breath.

"Malroy, where were you?" Smith asked.

"I was . . . with a lady friend, Sergeant," Malroy said as he paused and strapped in.

Corporal Seth Malroy was the youngest of the team at twenty-six years old. He was a lean guy who always hated weight lifting but loved to swim. His buzz-cut black hair used to be shaggy and long before he joined the military at age seventeen with his mother's consent. His baby blue eyes gave no indication of the things he had seen. He joined the military to find his way in life, and now was a ranking soldier in the Joint Task Force Two (JTF2) team. He was a very driven and self-disciplined man, but the other guys in his squad still called him a boy. After all these years in the military, Malroy still had no idea what he wanted out of life, but he felt at home with a rifle in his hand and his mates beside him in battle.

"You horndog," Sergeant Smith chuckled as he put his head back and closed his eyes.

"Hey," said Malroy. "When you have a job like ours, you have to seize every opportunity, if you know what I mean." Corporal Malroy winked.

"That'll change with marriage, buddy," Sergeant Smith said without opening his eyes.

Malroy laughed out loud. "Marriage—can I even *get* married nowadays?"

"You're right, you can't get married," said Smith. "Because no girl is crazy enough to marry you!"

Master Corporal Santos began to laugh as he covered his mouth.

"Oh, we all got jokes now, eh?" Malroy chuckled.

"Prepare for takeoff," the pilot said over the intercom.

Sergeant Major Black looked at all his men and nodded his head. Sergeant Smith was a combat engineer by trade, but he was also a vehicle technician from Bowmanville, where Sergeant Major Black grew up. Master Corporal Santos was a medical technician by trade, but he also specialized in policing and interrogation. Master Corporal Santos was from Quebec, and Corporal Malroy was from an artillery unit from Oshawa. Corporal Malroy had started off just loading shells into an artillery canon, but he worked and trained his way into the JTF2 team with his incredible weapons knowledge and fitness. Corporal Malroy's impressive reloading time was the fastest recorded time in the Canadian military. These four men made up the top company in the Canadian Forces today: the Black Fox Company. They had rescued 104 survivors, and their kills tallied over 600 infected and 17 berserkers.

The infected carried two viruses, with two modes of transmission. The Z2Z virus, carried in the saliva of all infected, turned healthy humans into infected crazies with a bite. The Z2B virus, however, was a bit more complex; the Z2B was also carried by infected, but not all. Only some infected carried both viruses, which is why berserkers (as they were commonly known) were so uncommon. When bitten by an infected, a victim never knew if they would become a berserker or what the scientists termed a "common infected." In a study, the scientists at the United States Army Medical Research Institute of Infectious Diseases (USAMRIID) found that there seemed to be an incubation period after an infected was killed. The virus gave signs of surviving in an airborne state for approximately five minutes after its host was deceased. Unfortunately, this was not *always* the case, and scientists were still trying to figure out why.

No one could really tell who would become a berserker and who would be an infected; scientists had been studying the two strains of virus since day one, but they couldn't find any conclusive evidence to show why these two strains had mutated differently.

Berserkers were the infected population not driven by the thirst for blood. Once infected by the Z2B virus, healthy humans became stronger, faster, and raging mad as berserkers, driven to incessant rage and violence like a rabid wolf. There weren't many berserkers, but when you saw one, it was better to hide, or as the soldiers say, "Be sure to save a bullet for yourself." Berserkers all looked different due to self-mutilation; they were so destructive that they often ripped themselves apart until they found something or someone else to inflict pain upon.

The CH-124 Sea King helicopter lifted off for Vancouver International Airport, which was going to take them approximately forty to forty-five minutes. Their mission was to raid grocery stores and markets. The only two areas that were not declared safe zones yet were British Columbia and the Northwest Territories. The Canadian Forces were working day in and day out to clear them out, but it seemed like a never-ending battle. The military had taken the airport and some surrounding buildings and established a perimeter guarding the base, but they still made countless attempts to clear more land.

"Alright, boys, here's the plan," Sergeant Major Black said as he stood up. "We land at YVR, and from there we have five other units joining us. They are gathering food, medical supplies, etcetera. We, on the other hand, have a special mission, and that is a rescue. Home base in Ottawa has been getting the US to fly drones over the greater Vancouver area, and they found an SOS on the top of a roof exactly 3.2 klicks from the grocery store that the other units are raiding. We have orders to check it out, rescue any survivors, and get back to safety with minimal to no attention drawn to ourselves."

After Sergeant Major Black had finished, the men all started loading their magazines into their weapons and mentally preparing themselves.

Smith looked around at the men he had fought alongside for so long. Their faces were stone cold, and their eyes empty—these men had fought so hard, never giving up on any shred of hope. And here they were again, risking their lives to give some person or persons a shred of hope in the darkness that had descended upon this new world. Smith always thought he would be retired, sitting on a beach with his wife, Linda, and his children. His biggest fear wasn't not making it home, but rather turning into one of the monsters he fought day in and day out before he got there.

Malroy finished loading and readying his weapons when he looked over at Master Corporal Santos; he was such a quiet man, humble in every way. Malroy never knew a man who prayed for the people he had killed. Santos was a warrior through and through, but he maintained his heart of gold, if that were possible, praying every night for the men he had taken from this world, then thanking god for keeping his life one more day.

Santos leaned over to Malroy. "You look scared today, little brother."

Malroy chuckled. "If anyone is scared it's you, big brother."

Santos and Malroy had formed such a bond that sometimes they thought they had been brothers in a past life. When Malroy first started in the military, he met Master Corporal Santos during the first aid courses that Santos was teaching. Then, years later, on their first mission together, Malroy was pinned down under fire and radioed in to leave him, and the one man's voice that came over the radio was Master Corporal Santos: "I'm not leaving you, little brother."

Master Corporal Santos threw smoke grenades and told Malroy to run. Without thinking, Malroy got up and began to run through the smoke. He heard gunfire, but it wasn't enemy fire; it was Santos covering him as he ran. Master Corporal Santos had pinpointed all the enemy locations and began to pick them off as Malroy ran toward him.

From that moment, they had always been within earshot of each other.

***

Forty minutes later, the CH-124 Sea King began its decent to the landing pad in the back of the Vancouver International Airport. The air never seemed to change anywhere you went; there was always that smell of death—rotting corpses and the dashed hopes of so many. After landing, the men attended to their gear until a convoy of Humvees and tanks came toward them. A man jumped out of the front Humvee and saluted Sergeant Major Black.

"At ease, Private," Sergeant Major Black commanded.

"Yes, sir. Here is your vehicle."

"Yes, thank you," Black said.

"Good luck, sir!" said the private, running to the Humvee behind and jumping in.

Corporal Malroy walked over to the Humvee's back passenger door and reached for the handle when a young man came up to him.

"Corporal Malroy, Private Brian Waters reporting for duty. I just wanted to say that it will be an honor to fight next to you today," said Waters. "You and your team are an inspiration to all of us to keep fighting." Waters extended his hand.

Corporal Malroy smiled and shook his hand.

"We are all inspirations to each other, Private Waters," said Malroy. "We all fight the same war. We are no different."

Private Waters smiled and began to walk away, but then he turned back. "You got my six, Corporal Malroy?"

"Always, Private Waters." And with that, Corporal Malroy got into the Humvee.

Sergeant Major Black got in the driver seat of the beige Canadian Forces Humvee, Smith got in the passenger seat, Malroy got on the machine gun that was attached to the roof, and Santos sat in the back.

Malroy loaded the belt into the gun and cocked it. "Let's roll!" he roared.

Sergeant Major Black looked over at Sergeant Smith. "Let's do this"

Smith nodded and fist-bumped Sergeant Major Black.

The convoy started rolling, and the guards opened the gates toward the barren city of Vancouver. The convoy moved through the streets slowly and silently, dodging flipped cars and rubble on the ground. Windows were smashed and small fires were still burning. Some buildings looked ready to collapse. Continuing toward the target, Corporal Malroy smacked the top of the Humvee and Sergeant Major Black stopped, stopping the whole convoy.

"Target, three o'clock, range 150 meters," Malroy said.

Sergeant Major Black parked and slowly got out, grabbing his sniper rifle and silencer. Black was known for his one-shot kill streak. He had started his career as a simple infantry soldier, digging holes and helping in the construction of bases in Afghanistan. He moved through the ranks fast, gathering himself a Sacrifice Medal and the

Command Commendation—a very high award given to a man or woman who goes beyond the call of duty. Sergeant Major Black got this award when he and his unit were under fire, and two of his six men were wounded and could not move. The command was to leave them, but Black carried both men on his back to safety, all the while getting shot in the leg. Sergeant Major Black was a well-known man within the Canadian military for leaving no one behind. Dead or alive, Black's motto was, "If you fight for the Canadian military and die, you will be buried in Canadian soil." After all the awards and recognition, the military sent Black to Military College, where he advanced further, eventually earning the rank of Sergeant Major; thus, they called him "Major" for short.

He screwed the silencer on, adopted the prone position, extended the bipod, and adjusted his scope. Taking aim, he took a deep breath, slowly exhaled, and then held his breath. He then gently squeezed the trigger with the pad of his index finger, like he had done count-less other times. The infected stopped and slowly turned towards the convoy of seven vehicles. Corporal Malroy put up his hand and raised his middle finger at the infected as Sergeant Major Black took the shot. The bullet entered the infected's left eye socket, burrowed through the few remaining functional parts of its brain, and exited via the occipital bone, shredding the skull like a head of lettuce. Black stepped back into the Humvee, handed his rifle to Sergeant Smith, and signaled to move forward with the mission.

Bodies covered the streets like blades of grass in a field. Blood covered the walls, vehicles, street signs, and the streets themselves. A horrid smell invaded the noses of the soldiers as they slowly moved through the city. Corporal Malroy reached for his gas mask, which was clipped to his backpack, and fixed it to his face to try and get away from the stench. Sergeant Smith looked out his window at the hell that surrounded him and his fellow teammates.

"You know, I always wanted to see Vancouver," he said, looking around.

Black looked at his sergeant.

"Welcome," he said sarcastically.

The convoy continued down the street toward the grocery store. They drove over what one might have once thought were speed bumps, but in reality, they were bodies. The grocery store came into view, so Black stopped the convoy and they formed up to move in on foot.

"Okay, Black Fox Company is moving to secondary target 'blue ribbon.' The rest of you hit the grocery store and be careful, be silent, and be calm," Sergeant Major Black said as he nodded to the men.

Private Waters looked over at Corporal Malroy.

"See you later, eh?" he said, walking with his unit.

"Yeah, man, stay classy," Malroy said.

Sergeant Major Black, Sergeant Smith, Corporal Malroy, and Master Corporal Santos held their rifles up and started their walk toward the target. Sergeant Major Black came to a corner and held up his fist, stopping the patrol. Sergeant Major Black peered around the corner and saw nothing. Waiting a moment, Sergeant Major Black looked around, and then waved his squad forward. Corporal Malroy silently sprinted to the next building across the street and looked around. Malroy gave the thumbs up for Smith and Santos to come. Both silently sprinted across the street, followed by Sergeant Major Black. Walking silently in single file for three hundred meters, the elite soldiers scanned all directions. Suddenly, Sergeant Major Black stopped again and waved to the ground, signaling everyone to get down. An infected came out from a building in the distance, followed shortly by two more. Black signaled toward a building across the street. Malroy and Smith stayed low, scurrying to the damaged building. They looked around, and then signaled back "all clear." Sergeant Major Black quickly followed.

"Three targets, middle of the street, no berserkers," Malroy said, lowering his binoculars.

"Blue ribbon, 1.1 klicks," Santos said, inspecting the map.

Sergeant Major Black looked around once more to ensure it was just the three infected in the area and gave the nod to Santos Malroy. They raised their C8 carbines with their silencer attachments, took aim at the three infected, and eliminated them simultaneously.

Sergeant Major Black waved his hand forward, and they all pushed on toward the target building. Pressed up against the wall, Black nodded to Smith. Sergeant Smith nodded back as he stepped back and kicked the door in. Black and Malroy entered, carbines raised, looking up and down, left to right. Santos followed Malroy, then Smith, who then tried shutting the off-hinged door behind them. This was an unnecessary action, since it immediately fell off the hinges. A red emergency light lit up the hallways.

Sergeant Major Black pointed up, signaling to head up to the roof. The hallways were littered with garbage. A couple bodies lay leaning against the wall. One body appeared to have been split open, spraying blood on the walls. The smell could make even a mortician vomit. Luckily for the Black Fox Company, they were equipped with gas masks to filter out any airborne virus and help cut the smell somewhat. They were not fazed by their physical surroundings—disregarding torn up bodies had become second nature. Some doors were busted open, off their hinges, some still locked. Other doors were half ripped up, covered in nail scratches. The fire alarm emitted a very faint high-pitched tone, since it had been active for months, and it barely worked now.

The exit sign on the darkened red ceiling was half hanging by some cords attached to the roof. Although there was darkness, the summer heat did not help the smell.

"Stay quiet, men, we don't want an infected horde disrupting this operation," Black whispered over the earpiece radios.

Malroy and Smith took the left staircase and headed towards the roof. Malroy walked up with his carbine pointed toward the next set of stairs they would have to climb, while Smith watched their backs as they ascended to the roof. Black and Santos went to the

11

right and up the staircase. The staircase was grimy and smelled of mothballs with the bitter scent of rotting bodies. The masks helped, but death still smelled like death. A faint redness lit the staircase, but it got darker as they progressed to the roof. Black and Santos headed up, faster and faster up the stairs, until Black put up his fist, signaling them to stop. There was a whimpering from the eighth-floor corridor.

"I got something, eighth floor, sounds like crying," Black said as he signaled Santos to go through the door.

Santos pulled the door slowly open and Black proceeded through the dark corridor. Santos followed with his left hand on Black's left shoulder. Malroy and Smith came from the other end of the hallway and saw Santos and Black. The crying got louder and louder, when suddenly an infected came from an apartment on the left side of the hallway and charged at Malroy. Malroy put two bullets into the infected's head and its knees buckled, dropping right at Malroy's feet.

Everyone paused, and then quickly moved toward the blood curdling screams.

The team ran to the crying sound, meeting in the middle of the corridor. Malroy found a door and he kicked it in. Black and the others charged through. A woman in her early thirties with light skin and bright red hair had her arms wrapped around a little boy who had the look of pure terror on his face. They were huddled in the corner of the room. Food wrappers covered the floor. A man lay face down on the floor with a bullet wound exiting the back of his head; his hand was extended toward the mother, as if he had been reaching for her when he was shot.

"Infected? Or murder?" Malroy asked

The woman slowly raised her head and stared at Malroy.

"Infected," she said in a soft but angered tone.

"We need to move now, ma'am," Black said as he extended his hand.

The mother, in shock, kept her head down and arms wrapped around her seven-year-old son. Her bright hair covered her face. She looked weak, malnourished. Her clothes were dirty and torn, as if she had been grabbed by the collar. Her child looked up at Black and tugged on his mother's arm with what looked like excitement.

"Ma'am," Black repeated louder this time. "We need to move now!"

The mother sat still. When Smith grabbed her arms, she began to thrash and scream, but Smith managed to get the boy and hand him to Malroy. Smith then gathered the struggling mother who lunged at Malroy, trying to get her son. Malroy turned his back as the woman jumped on him; Smith grabbed the frantic woman off Malroy's back and hugged her in his arms.

"Ma'am, we are here to help," he said sternly. "My name is Sergeant Brock Smith, and we are here to rescue you and your son. Please calm down."

The woman, after a moment, began to calm down, and then suddenly became weak and collapsed in Smith's arms.

Then sounds of breaking glass and roars filled the eardrums of everyone in the room.

"Convoy to Black Fox Company," said a radio tech. "You have a horde coming your way, moving in fast."

"Copy that," said Black as he signaled to move to the roof access staircase.

Smith and Malroy fled to the roof, leading the pack with the seven-year-old boy and his mother in their arms as Santos and Black took up defensive positions behind them. Infected began pouring out of the stairwell and down the corridor. Black and Santos began eliminating the infected in batches of controlled burst of fire from their C8s.

Malroy got to the roof access door, quickly dropping his shoulder and protecting the boy with his body. He smashed into the door, opening it abruptly. Smith quickly followed as he and Malroy both freed their hands and began to cover Black and Santos as they ran up the stairs, fleeing the infected. Once through the door, Santos slammed it shut and braced it, digging his heels into the gravel-topped roof.

"Convoy, where are the other units?" Sergeant Major Black asked, looking around.

"Back at convoy, waiting," Convoy replied.

"Can we get a chopper lift now? Tell them to go!" Sergeant Major Black demanded.

"Sea King will be there in five minutes," Convoy replied.

"We have—"

But Black was cut off by more loud groans of the infected charging down the street, and by the sounds of glass shattering at the bottom floor.

"Just hurry," Sergeant Major Black said as he reloaded a magazine into his carbine and pointed it at the door.

"Stay calm, little brother. Now is not the time," Santos said calmly.

Malroy shook his hand and readjusted his aim.

The deep groans got closer and closer. There were screeches and windows smashing as the horde got into the building. A bead of sweat rolled down Sergeant Smith's face as he looked at the two survivors. Once again, he and his team were a symbol of hope they had never asked to be—they were now all that these two survivors had.

Smith turned his back to the streets and aimed his gun at the door. "Assume it's just us men, we can't hope for a chopper now."

Then a helicopter was heard in the distance. Sergeant Smith turned and saw the helicopter coming.

"One minute out!" Smith yelled.

Smith began to get the survivors ready for a quick extraction. Santos and Malroy held the door shut with all their strength as more and more infected piled on the other side. The Sea King began to hover close to the roof as Smith opened the helicopter's door and saw other survivors inside.

"No room, just take the survivors!" Sergeant Smith said as he helped the mother and boy into the helicopter.

The pilot nodded. "Tell your men to release the door on my signal, and we'll give those infected something to chew on." And with that, the co-pilot left his chair and manned the machine gun.

Smith signaled Black to move as the co-pilot took aim. The pilot gave the thumbs up. Santos and Malroy quickly released the door and dove to either side as the ringing sound of the machine gun began and bullets pounded the door opening. Infected began to get ripped apart by the machine gun fire, bodies falling backwards down the stairs as the rain of empty bullet casings landed on the roof of the ten-story apartment building. Black crouched behind a mid-sized ventilation system while the slaughter occurred, pointing his carbine at the door, watching for any infected that might break free from the machine gun fire.

Once the machine gun ran empty, Black Fox company recovered and pointed their carbines at the doorway, which now looked like a slaughter house floor, drenched in blood with body parts everywhere and guts hanging from bodies.

"Cheers, mate, takeoff now," Black instructed as the pilot saluted and took off, taking the survivors back to the base. "Control, this is Sergeant Major Black, we require another extraction ASAP."

Sergeant Major Black was standing still for a second, looking out at the chaotic city of Vancouver, when he heard a honk followed by shots going off. "What was that?" He looked over the ledge and saw the convoy.

"We leave no man behind!" Private Waters hollered, gunning down a group of seven infected.

"Rappel down," Black said as he reached in his pack and released his ropes from his gear.

As most of the team began to pull out their rappelling lines, two infected came thrashing through the door. Sergeant Major Black instinctively reached for his Browning 9 mm pistol and shot both in the head.

Black helped tie off the ropes and gave the thumbs up. Santos and Smith went first, Malroy guiding and anchoring the weight for them. Then a loud bang was heard deep in the darkness of the corridor.

"Faster!" Black yelled as he grabbed his carbine and aimed it at the door.

Smith tugged on the rope to signal they were safely on the ground.

"Sergeant Major Black, let's go!" Malroy yelled.

Black whipped his carbine around onto his back and grabbed the end of the rope

"You need an anchor! Go!" Sergeant Major Black ordered. Malroy stared for a second, and then heard another bang and growing roars.

"You can come, too!" Corporal Malroy yelled.

"Go! That's an order," Black said, looking back at the doorway and pointing his weapon.

Malroy started to rappel down as Black wrapped and tied the rope around his waist, grabbed his rifle again, and aimed it at the doorway. Infected began running out. Sergeant Major Black fired shot after shot, aiming for the heads and staying focused and calm as he gunned down infected. Living infected tripped over the dead ones, falling like flies. Black's focus was unbreakable—it was like nothing else was happening as he focused in on one infected after the other—until he felt a tug on his waist from the rope, signaling that Malroy was down. Black fired off a couple more rounds then slung his weapon onto his back and held his legs together in one motion, causing the rope to fall to the ground. Black quickly picked up the tied rope and ran for the edge. At the last moment, he jumped off the ledge and tossed the tied end of the rope, hooking it around the ventilation system he had previously crouched behind, hoping it was solid enough. In midair, Black grabbed the rope in one hand, pulled out his pistol with the other, and shot the two infected that had chased him off the roof. Black slammed into the side of the apartment building, losing his grip but quickly regaining it. His shoulder throbbed with pain as he rappelled down the rope.

As Black landed on top of the tank, Smith roared, "All clear!"

The front Humvee heard the sergeant's command and began to press forward, back to the base.

Sergeant Major Black's hands trembled, his heart pounded in his chest, and his shoulder throbbed with pain as Sergeant Smith steadied him on the roof of the tank.

"Are you okay, Major?" Malroy asked with a worried tone.

"I'll be fine, just a little scratch," Black said with some pain in his tone.

The convoy moved through the streets, the tank desecrating the horde of infected as they drove off. Once they were at a safe distance, they got Sergeant Smith, Corporal Malroy, Master Corporal Santos, and Sergeant Major Black off the roof of the tank to quickly move them into the Humvees. They all jumped down and scurried for the Humvees. Once all in, they quickly began moving down the street again when all of a sudden, a berserker came darting from an alleyway and slammed into the side of the Humvee that Private Waters was in.

Corporal Malroy's eyes widened as he tried desperately to pull his sidearm out of its holster. The berserker smashed the window and began to violently pull Private Waters out of the small Humvee window. A couple soldiers shot off some rounds but missed as the berserker tackled Waters to the ground and clawed at his face. Corporal Malroy sprang out of his Humvee and opened fire, shooting the berserker six times in the head as it became limp on top of Private Waters.

"No!" Malroy roared as he knelt over Waters. "Brian!" he said, studying his body.

Private Waters' arms quickly started to turn a light red color, almost like a rash, and his blue veins began to bulge and turn a vibrant blue.

"He's turning!" a soldier cried.

Corporal Malroy stood up and looked at the horde coming their way.

"Sorry, brother," Corporal Malroy said as he got back into his Humvee.

As they drove off, Malroy heard a single shot that he knew was now located in Private Waters' skull. Malroy stared out of the window, looking around at the streets, Waters' screams still ringing in his ears as he tried to focus on the surroundings he was currently in. Malroy had never seen a man get ripped apart like that before. Sure, he had seen his fair share of unspeakable things, but seeing that berserker in action was a first for him.

Moments later, more gunshots were heard, and more infected were dying. On a certain level, it wasn't always easy to kill an infected; if it were a child who had been infected and you had to eliminate the target, the hesitation was still there. Some days it felt like the cure—if eventually there was one—couldn't come soon enough, especially when faced with putting down an infected child or woman.

Vancouver used to be such a vibrant city in Canada, but now, during the reclaim phase of the military's plan to combat the infected, it occurred to most who fought in the city that it would never be the same. This epidemic was going to be a permanent scar that the human race would never forget—some thought, in fact, that the human race would never recover.

Going over the bridge on Gilbert Road, Master Corporal Santos saw bodies drifting in the Fraser River, lifeless and pale: a slight reminder of the hell that had come upon them. Turning off Russ Baker Way onto Grant McConachie Way toward the airport, everyone was quiet. Not a word was spoken, besides the odd shot fired at an infected.

***

Malroy's mind went blank when they got back to the base. Santos opened the door as Malroy sat there, staring forward.

Santos gestured with his hand. "Come on, little brother. Let's get cleaned up."

Malroy paused before slowly bowing his head. "I told him I had his six, Andy." Malroy continued his blank stare.

Santos reached in the Humvee and put his hand on Malroy's shoulder. Malroy shook him off. "I told him I had his six, and now he's dead." There was anger in his tone.

"It's not your fault, Seth," Santos said, holding Malroy tighter.

Santos was continuing to comfort Malroy when they overheard a group of soldiers. "Did you guys see Brian? Damn, dude, he got messed up eh!"

Malroy's eyes widened as he pushed Santos off of him and exited the Humvee.

Santos quickly tried to grab Malroy, but missed. "*Corporal* Malroy, no!"

Malroy now speed walking over to the group. "Yeah, he got messed up, eh?" He reached the group and pushed the first soldier.

"Hey man, calm down," the soldier said, raising his hands.

Corporal Malroy grabbed the soldier and punched him square in the face, causing the soldier to fall. Corporal Malroy landed on the soldier, and was about to ground and pound him when Master Corporal Santos wrapped his arms around Corporal Malroy.

"This isn't your fight, Seth," Santos said as he ripped Malroy off the man and guided him away from the group.

Once they were far enough away, Santos stopped Malroy, turned him around, and then slapped him hard across the right cheek.

"Get a hold of yourself, little brother," Santos said. "These things are going to happen. They suck. I know that. But you can't waste your energy fighting our own. Private Waters is gone, and nothing will bring him back. Accept that here and now so we can move on together."

Malroy stood, his jaw clenched.

"It was not your fault, Corporal Malroy," said Santos. "This is what happens in war. We know this all too well."

Santos placed his hand on Malroy's shoulder.

"I'm sorry. I know, I just . . . Sometimes it's too much," Malroy said, bowing his head in defeat.

"Never apologize, little brother. We are taking on more than we are built for. Have your outburst, get the emotions out, but always remember we are in this together. I need you strong and calm-minded, and you need me strong and calm-minded, okay?" Santos said as he began to walk away.

"I understand," Malroy said softly.

***

Sergeant Major Black and Sergeant Smith entered the control tent and looked over at Hopkins, the base colonel.

"Sir, did the survivors make it home okay?" Sergeant Smith asked, he and Black standing at attention.

"At ease, gentleman, I appreciate the work you did today. All the survivors are accounted for and are getting examined as we speak in the secure quarantine tent. They will be watched for twenty-four hours, and then we can send them to the safe haven," Colonel Hopkins said, looking down at some papers.

"Where did the other survivors come from, sir? We were told there was only one rescue mission," Sergeant Major Black said.

"From what Captain Stokely reported, he was waiting for your signal for extraction when he saw a group of five on an adjacent rooftop. We sent him in to pick them up and then you guys," Colonel Hopkins said.

"The more the merrier—right, sir?" Sergeant Smith said.

"In these times, gentleman, the more infected dead and more survivors saved the better," said the commander. "You boys did great work today, as usual. Day in and day out, you men prove to the whole Canadian Military why the Black Fox Company is the best around."

"Thank you, sir," Sergeant Major Black said as he stood at attention and saluted.

"Dismissed," Colonel Hopkins said.

2. AMERICAN WAY

Two men in uniform walked into the White House. One man held a black briefcase in his right hand as they walked toward the Oval Office. The man with the briefcase had short, properly groomed blond hair. He was clean-shaven, and he was much lankier than the other man, who was burlier and dressed in tactical gear with a handgun on his hip.

Two secret service guards armed with assault rifles and pistols stood in front of the door. The two men approached the guards and handed them their badges. The one guard swiped the two badges through a machine that indicated who the two men were. The screen flashed "Dr. Clase" and his bodyguard, "Corporal Rex Witter." Both American soldiers, Dr. Clase was a military scientist trying to figure this infection out, working among other scientists who were also looking for a cure. Corporal Rex Witter was a Navy Seal assigned to protect Dr. Clase when he traveled through America. Throughout the nation, America was still not fully cleared of the infection. California, Texas, Alabama, Louisiana, Georgia, Arkansas, Mississippi, and Florida were still considered hot zones.

Dr. Clase walked up to the President's desk and laid his briefcase down.

"Good morning, Dr. Clase," the President greeted.

"Good morning, Mr. President," Dr. Clase said. "Sir, I need more human specimens. I feel I am very close to some type of cure that can kill this virus once and for all, but I need more humans for testing. The lab animals are showing promising signs, but I need more human results to be sure."

President Frank D. Gallagher leaned back in his chair, rubbing his face in deep thought. The President looked exhausted and mentally drained from all the chaos that had come during his term of leadership. He looked physically drained, with an almost sickly paleness to his body. He moved from his chair, slowly looking out the window at Washington and his district. Buildings were damaged, dirt had become the new grass, and the cleanup of the nation could only stretch so far.

"Everyone leave except Dr. Clase," the President ordered.

When the room had cleared, he turned to the scientist. "Dr. Clase, I am cutting resources to your experiments. I can no longer condone your methods with human experiments. If people find out what I have given blessing to, people won't trust the government anymore, and the last thing I need is the people to turn on me while this mess is going on," the President said as he bowed his head.

Dr. Clase stood there, shocked by the words that the President spoke.

"What do you *mean*? We had a deal!" Dr. Clase demanded. "There are human lives at risk—the world as we know it could be lost if no one finds a cure, and you are cutting my resources!" Dr. Clase slammed his hands on the desk.

"If you need live specimens, you have to get them yourself. I cannot be associated anymore, and neither can the US government," the President said.

"You can't *do* this—I am close to a breakthrough. I could be the one to save this world from absolute shit, and you handcuff me when I'm so close. You think the other idiots at USAMRIID are close?" Dr. Clase huffed.

"I told you to *share* your finding with everyone," President Gallagher said, glaring at the man in front of him. "In fact, I *ordered* you to!"

"This is *my* work. I told you I will find the cure, but on my terms! Now I need human specimens. Are you going to give them to me or not? It's not like anyone will miss them—they are degenerates," Dr. Clase said calmly.

"It's not right, Dr. Clase. Now leave!" And with that, the President waved Dr. Clase out of his office.

Dr. Clase grabbed his briefcase and stormed out of the Oval Office, followed by Corporal Rex Witter.

Walking out of the White House, Dr. Clase got in the car and looked at Corporal Witter. "When do you leave me and go back to your unit?" Dr. Clase asked in an angry tone.

"I leave when you are secure again," Corporal Witter said, starting the black unmarked SUV vehicle.

"Head to my personal lab in Bethesda," Dr. Clase ordered. Corporal Rex Witter looked at Dr. Clase in shock.

"Yes, sir," Corporal Witter said.

"I am close to finding what makes them snap, but I need a couple more specimens. If the President tells me to go get my own, I will!" Dr. Clase said in a fit of anger.

Corporal Witter looked at Dr. Clase. "If you want more specimens, I can call my unit so we do it safely," Corporal Witter said.

"Perfect, we will go to my lab, and you can make some calls from the landline there—but it doesn't reach too far with some of the satellites down," Dr. Clase said.

"Satellites are down? I thought communication wasn't an issue," Corporal Witter asked.

"Sorry, not down. NASA has designated some to strictly digital photo ops for tracking the infected and their movements, as well as to see what cities are hotspots, and how the other bases are doing.

Simply put, they have some satellites nicknamed 'God's Eyes.' The other ones are for communication."

"Understood—they are located at JB Anacostia-Bolling," Corporal Witter said sternly.

***

When they arrived at the lab, Corporal Rex Witter parked in front. The building looked very new and modern. It was built right before the outbreak happened and was heavily protected.

"Doesn't look like anything happened to *this* building," Corporal Witter said, getting out of the vehicle.

"Yes, it was guarded well," Dr. Clase said, scanning his badge and then scanning his eye for security clearance.

Both men entered the lab as the two steel doors slammed shut behind them.

"The phone is over there," Dr. Clase pointed.

Corporal Witter walked over to the phone, sat down, and began to make calls to his Commander. Dr. Clase placed his briefcase on the desk surface and opened it by entering a four-digit code. He reached in and grabbed a vial of blue liquid and placed it in what looked to be a high-tech mini-fridge. He then grabbed his notes and jotted down the name of the vial's contents onto a tag, and then above it he wrote the word "Oval." He wrapped the tag around the vial and put a hazardous symbol on it.

I'll show you, Mr. President, Dr. Clase thought.

Corporal Rex Witter got up from the chair and looked over at Dr. Clase. "They are coming. Should be about twenty minutes, my commander said," Corporal Witter explained.

"That's great. Who is coming?" Dr. Clase asked.

"My commander, Sergeant Delmore. My brother, Corporal Ryan Witter, and finally Master Corporal Eddie Kilghannon," Witter replied.

***

Half an hour past, and then Corporal Rex Witter started chuckling.

"What's so funny?" Dr. Clase asked.

"Do you hear that?" Corporal Witter said.

Dr. Clase looked around, trying to hear something, but he heard nothing.

"I don't hear a thing," Dr. Clase explained.

Then a deep laugh filled the room and Master Corporal Kilghannon walked in. Dr. Clase was in shock at the size of this man; he was six foot three, and looked to be 230 lbs of beer and muscles. He had buzzed red hair and a red goatee, along with scars all up his arms, and a scar that went from the left corner of his left eye down his left cheek and ended at his jawline. Corporal Ryan Witter and Sergeant Delmore came in after Master Corporal Kilghannon and stood beside Corporal Rex Witter.

"This is my team," Corporal Rex Witter said. "This is my brother, Corporal Ryan Witter, Sergeant Fred Delmore, and Master Corporal Eddie Kilghannon." Corporal Witter pointed to each one as he introduced them.

Dr. Clase, unable to move, was in shock. "I've . . . I've never felt so safe in a room before!" he stuttered. All the men laughed.

Master Corporal Kilghannon walked over to Dr. Clase and gripped his shoulder. "Nothing's touching our scientist friend," he said. He had a pronounced Irish accent. Then he let go of Dr. Clase's shoulder. "You got any beer? Seems to be hard to come by."

"Uh, no, sorry, but we do have straight laboratory alcohol if you'd like," Dr. Clase said with a bit of hesitation.

"Hey, I'm no alcoholic!" Kilghannon said with a serious face, holding it for a moment and then cracking a smile.

"I'm just kidding! Lighten up, ya bastard," the master corporal laughed.

After all the introductions, the men gathered up their gear and headed out the door to the Humvee that was parked out front. Master Corporal Kilghannon and Corporal Ryan Witter packed the Humvee and got into the backseat with Dr. Clase, who was gripping his laptop with both hands.

"You scared, lad?" Kilghannon asked as he laughed and smacked Dr. Clase on the back.

Sergeant Delmore put the Humvee in drive and began their drive to the airbase. Washington looked grim: kids walking with their heads down, still scared; people openly robbing broken-into stores and taking what was left of the stock; bodies still lying in alleyways. The cleanup squads did the best they could to clear away everything, but too much destruction had been done. All of America was trying to recover, but the path to recovery seemed endless. Dr. Clase remembered the trees that had lined the streets downtown, and the culture and atmosphere of Washington before the infection had broke out. Now, Washington was a barren land that seemed to be under construction, but there were barely any workers left to rebuild it. The buildings were barely holding their own structures, the smell of death was rife in the streets, and the neighborhoods were abandoned . . . It would seem that everyone had taken the feeling of "home" for granted. Now, in this day and age of the infection, "home" was a feeling that had faded for everyone, and the possibility that it would never return was a true fear.

They arrived at the airbase, handing all their badges over and getting scanned in.

"Any helicopters available for getting specimens?" Sergeant Delmore asked the guard.

"We have twelve left that are allotted for special duties. Do you require a pilot?" the guard asked.

"They got me," Sergeant Delmore said.

Sergeant Delmore was a seasoned flyer. He had started in the Air Force, but got sick of seeing men fighting on the ground and dying and not being able to help, so he stopped flying and joined the Navy Seals so he could be helpful deep in the action.

The gate opened, and Sergeant Delmore continued toward the helipads. The base seemed empty, with all the available soldiers out fighting in the hot-zone states, trying to extinguish the infected. The lack of fuel was a big fear. Many aircrafts were now grounded unless authorized for use, because they took too much to fill up. Minimal aircrafts were used. Vehicles were on a very tight use policy.

Dr. Clase got in the front seat of the helicopter and put his headset on.

"Okay, we have room for three specimens. Is that going to be enough?" Sergeant Delmore asked.

Dr. Clase nodded and gave the thumbs up. Everybody strapped in and gave the thumbs up for the helicopter to lift off.

***

About half an hour into the flight, Dr. Clase looked down at the wasteland of America. He could see groups of infected walking lifelessly around in the streets, looking for food. Dr. Clase then noticed a fast-moving object that jumped at an infected, ripped its head off, and tossed it like a soccer ball.

"Is that a berserker?" Dr. Clase yelled.

"Yes, sir! You don't want to be stuck with them in a room!" Delmore laughed.

"The Berserker's look different on the outside of a lab?" Dr. Clase asked.

"They kill anything. That one will probably die soon—he attacked a horde of infected, the others will see him and kill him once they get a hold of him," Ryan Witter explained.

"Keep your eyes open for a lone wolf infected walking around," Delmore ordered.

Ryan Witter looked out his window and saw a group of four infected that were just behind a building, away from the horde.

"Sir, four stinkers behind the plaza, near the 'Smoke for 2' store."

"Okay," said Delmore, "drop the ropes, get the gag-mask guns, and bring them home."

The Witter brothers dropped the ropes from the helicopter and hooked themselves in.

"You have three minutes before that horde gets over here, boys, so make it quick," Delmore said as he waved his hand down. Then he concentrated on holding the helicopter steady enough for them to drop.

The Witters rappelled down the ropes and hit the ground. The four infected looked over and then started charging at them. Master Corporal Kilghannon shot one of the infected in the head from the helicopter. Ryan Witter pulled out the gag-mask gun and shot a bullet that opened into a small netted mask that wrapped around the infected's mouth and locked behind its head. Rex Witter shot the other infected, and then both men shot ropes around the two infected's' ankles, causing them to fall. The third infected got closer and closer when Rex Witter made a fist and smashed it into the infected's face, knocking it down. Then he shot the gag-mask around the infected's face and cuffed it.

"All clear. Sending the stinks up," Corporal Rex Witter said as he and his brother hooked them into the ropes.

"Who thought we would be doing this three years ago, eh, Rex?" Ryan Witter laughed as he tied the knot.

The infected's thrashed and tossed, so Rex Witter smacked them with the blunt end of his gun, knocking them out.

"What . . . they are still alive," Corporal Rex Witter smirked at Dr. Clase

Kilghannon manned the machine and started pulling the infected up. Dr. Clase looked out his window and saw a figure moving faster and faster through the crowd of infected.

"Guys . . ." Dr. Clase said, but no one answered. "Oh my god, berserker!" he yelled over the radio.

Corporal Rex Witter pulled out his gun and turned around to see a berserker charging him. The berserker smashed into him, knocking him down to the ground. Ryan pulled out his gun, but the berserker was too fast and jumped on his back. Fighting back, Ryan grabbed the berserker's head and flipped him off his back, then he regained himself as the berserker got to its feet.

In the helicopter, Sergeant Delmore opened a container, got a rifle, and passed it to Dr. Clase. "Cover them!"

Dr. Clase looked at Sergeant Delmore, completely clueless about how to operate the weapon.

"Did you not do basic training?" Sergeant Delmore asked.

"I went right into the science sector—"

Master Corporal Kilghannon ripped the gun from Dr. Clase's hands. "Just push this button!"

Dr. Clase pressed the button faster and faster now, sweat beading down his face.

Rex Witter got to his feet and pulled out his knife, but then saw the horde of infected closing in on them.

"Ryan, get out of here!" Rex yelled as he pulled out his pistol and shot the berserker in the head.

"It's too late to be quiet now!" Rex Witter said as he started running.

Corporal Ryan Witter started to follow his brother as they ran through the grassy field with a horde of infected charging behind them.

"Keep going, little brother. Don't stop!" Rex Witter yelled.

Delmore flew after the Witter brothers, knowing that his margin of error was very slim now. Kilghannon was straining to pull the infected up into the bird.

"Get those goddamned specimens up here now, Master Corporal," Sergeant Delmore ordered.

Corporals Rex and Ryan Witter were running as fast as they could, dropping gear to lessen the weight, when finally, Dr. Clase got the infected into the helicopter and chained them up.

"They are in. Bring the men up now!" Dr. Clase yelled.

Dr. Clase dropped the ropes back down and got on the radio.

"Alright you two lunatics, grab the ropes and we will pull you up off the ground," Master Corporal Kilghannon explained.

"Copy that!" Corporal Ryan Witter said, frantically and out of breath as he continued to run.

Looking forward, Rex Witter saw a cliff coming up. The infected were gaining on him and his brother. He took out a grenade and pulled the pin. Meters away from the cliff, he threw the grenade back into the horde of infected and then faced forward. Corporals Rex and Ryan Witter ran as hard as they could then jumped off the cliff. The grenade exploded behind them, blood filling the air. They closed their mouths and eyes, but for a split-second Corporal Rex Witter opened his eyes to see a black rope in front of him. He grabbed at the rope, looked down, saw his brother's hand, and grabbed it. Then he closed his eyes and mouth as blood splattered everywhere.

"Don't move, boys, we got you," Sergeant Delmore said. "Just keep your mouths shut."

Delmore piloted the helicopter about a kilometer away to a safe zone and landed it gently.

Dr. Clase got out of the helicopter and ran over with a disinfectant towel to wipe off the infectious blood. The corporals got to their feet and rubbed their faces.

"Holy hell!" Ryan Witter yelled in excitement. "That was probably the crappiest moment in my life. Had to rely on Rex with his eyes closed, holding a rope with one hand."

Ryan Witter laughed as he rested his hands on his bent knees, spitting and catching his breath.

"Oh, please . . . I had this all under control!" Rex said, inhaling and exhaling deeply. He took a deep breath and looked around.

"How did you know there was going to be a rope for you to grab?" Dr. Clase asked.

"I didn't! I'm surprised to be alive," he laughed as he patted Dr. Clase on the back and walked toward the helicopter.

"Alright, boys and girls," said Delmore, "we are all good, so let's get these specimens back to the lab."

3. RUMORS

It was a humid summer night. A gentle gust blew through the base. Sergeant Major Black and Corporal Malroy walked to the only bar in the base that had barely anything so they could have a beer and meet up with Master Corporal Santos and Sergeant Smith. The base was quiet at night.

Black and Malroy walked into the bar and sat down with Santos and Smith.

"Gentlemen," Black said as he pulled his chair out.

"Gentlemen?" Sergeant Smith chuckled. "Have you seen what we do?"

Santos smiled at the comment and took a sip of his beer.

"It tastes better now, knowing it could be my last one," Santos said as he took another sip.

Sergeant Major Black went to the bar and got two beers from the bartender, who seemed shaken.

"Are you alright?" Black asked as he grabbed the beers.

The bartender looked around, and then back at Black. "Rumor has it that the infected are taking over, and there is no way for us to stop it," he said with fear in his voice.

"You don't say . . . Who said this?" Black asked.

33

"Heard it from a military buddy of mine," the bartender said as he gave his last beers to Black.

"I assure you, we are winning this fight," Black said as he picked up his beers and left.

"What was *that* about, Major?" Malroy asked as he grabbed his beer.

"Soldier's telling the base workers that we are losing the fight," Black answered.

"To the people we saved today," Smith toasted.

They all clanked glasses and chugged their beers.

"How ya doing, kid?" Smith asked Malroy.

"I'm alright, just a little off, I guess," Malroy said, looking down.

"It's not your fault, Seth, these things happen in our line of work," Black said, patting Malroy on the back.

"I should've had his back, though. He got us out of that situation, and what do I do to repay him? Let him get mauled by a berserker!" Malroy said, slamming his glass on the table.

"Hey, we did all that we could. You did your best today. The best thing to do now is honor Private Waters and fight on. It's what he, I, or anybody would want," Santos said, raising his glass. "To Brian."

All the men raised their glasses and finished what was left of their beers.

***

Later that night, after a couple beers, Sergeant Major Black stood up, said his goodbyes for the night, and left the bar to walk back to his barracks. He exited the bar and popped his collar to block the cool air from the back of his neck. Walking home, he stopped and looked around. Closing his eyes, he lifted his face to the sky and took a deep breath in.

Yelling and screams for help fill Albert Street in Ottawa. Car alarms blare. Explosions illuminate the night sky. Bodies lie mangled and battered on the ground. He fights with his unit: Sergeant Smith shooting infected after infected. Master Corporal Santos tending wounded people, Corporal Malroy watching over Sergeant Smith's back.

He looks around and sees a vehicle, the door swinging open.

"Follow me!" he yells.

Smith, Santos, and Malroy cover him as they make a bolt for the car. Infected are falling at their feet as they fire round after round into their skulls. He jumps into the front seat and sees the keys in the ignition.

"Everyone in!" he orders.

Smith and Malroy jump in the back and break the windows. Santos grabs the front seat as they speed off.

"Sergeant Major Black, what are we doing?" Santos asks.

"Saving our families!" he says and floors the vehicle toward a horde of infected.

"Hey man, are you okay?" Malroy said, catching up to Major on their way back from the bar.

Sergeant Major Black opened his eyes and came back to reality. "Yeah, just taking in the night air."

Black shook his head, and they both walked down the road and back to the base.

***

Sergeant Major Black reached his bunk and sat down on the hard cot, wishing he were back in his own bed. He looked around the plain grey room, which was almost so plain that it numbed his thoughts. His gear was placed in the bunk nicely to the left of his bed. The one tiny window in the wall let some moonlight into his room. He looked over at his gear and smirked at all the scrape marks, dirt, and dents in his chest plate armor. He rubbed his eyes as thoughts raced through his mind. He walked into the washroom and rested his hands on the sink as he stared at himself in the mirror. His deep green eyes used to be full of life, but now he looked at himself and found nothing looking back. His soul was gone. His heart was tarred black, and his emotions were numbed. His whole world was gone, his wife and daughter killed by the virus. Guilt ran through him like it was his own blood. Major John Black stood up and examined his war-ridden body. Scars, bruises, and scrapes covered him like a map of the life he had lived in all the wars he had fought.

"Who am I?" he whispered to himself, fingering the cross that his wife once wore. "Why didn't you take me?"

A burst of rage started in his chest as he punched the mirror, glass shattering as the warm blood started down his throbbing hand. He bowed his head and turned the tap on to wash the blood away.

The room was cold and plain as he got into his night attire and pulled the covers over himself. Shutting his eyes, he fell asleep instantly and was out for the night.

Smith and Malroy jump in the back and break the windows.

"Sergeant Major Black," Santos asks, "what are we doing?"

"Saving our families!" Black says as he accelerates toward a horde of infected. Infected bodies smash against the car as he floors the gas pedal. Smith and Malroy hold on to the handles above the back windows as the car jerks around.

He clears the horde and continues driving out of the city and toward the military housing neighborhood. The car is silent, all men thinking about their families: Smith's pregnant wife, Santos' wife, and Black's own wife and baby daughter. Malroy is single and has no one back home; the military is Seth Malroy's new family.

Black drives through the iron gate and stops the car. The neighborhood is barren and empty.

"Maybe they got evacuated, Major," Malroy says, looking around.

Then they see an infected walk out from behind a house that looks to be torn to shreds. Black grabs his rifle and gets out of the car and starts to run in the direction of his home.

The infected looks over at him, but he shoots it in the head as he runs by. Malroy, Smith, and Santos get out of the car and follow him. Bodies are scattered all over the neighborhood, blood turning the grass red, and windows are smashed. A woman lies dead in Black's driveway, but it is not his wife. He runs into his home, looking around.

"Lisa!"

Black jumped up from deep sleep covered in sweat, breathing fast with his heart pounding in his chest as he looked around and gathered himself. He slowed his breathing down and cradled his face in both his hands, groaning as he rubbed his eyes.

Then he slowly lay back in his cold, hard cot.

***

The next morning, Corporal Malroy woke up and felt the sun shining through the small window in his room. *Good morning, Hell.* He slowly opened his eyes and got to his feet and started stretching. A knock came at the door, and Sergeant Smith entered.

"The general wants us," Smith said, shutting the door.

Malroy threw a T-shirt and pants on and strapped his boots up tight in a hurry as he rushed out the door. Sergeant Major Black, Master Corporal Santos, and Sergeant Smith stood with arms crossed in a circle with General Davidson.

"What did I miss?" Malroy asked as he joined the circle.

"We are going to Washington. We are on security duty for the Prime Minister," Sergeant Smith said. Malroy looked around with a puzzled look.

"President Gallagher has requested the Prime Minister come to talk about a growing concern," said the general. "The President also asked for Canada's top task force, and so we put forward the Black Fox Company. You four men will guard the Prime Minister and get him home safely. Wheels up in one hour."

All four men nodded and saluted.

Walking away from the debriefing, they felt a knot growing in their stomachs. All the men went back to their bunks and got their gear prepped and ready. Sergeant Smith picked up his satellite phone and dialed the base in Manitoba.

The phone rang four times, and then a man answered the phone. "Master Corporal Cody, how can I help you?" the man greeted.

"This is Sergeant Brock Smith. I need extension 4934."

"One moment, Sergeant Smith."

The phone line started to ring again and again until a little voice picked the phone up.

"Hello?" a little girl said.

It was Brock Smith's daughter, Rose. He paused for a moment and held back his emotions. "Hey sweetheart, it's Daddy."

The little voice rose with excitement and then called out, "Mommy, Mommy, it's Daddy!"

He smiled, listening to his baby girl's voice call him "Daddy."

His wife, Linda, took the phone and put it on speaker. "Hey, honey, oh goodness I miss you like crazy!"

"I miss you both so much," he said. "And Daddy is coming home soon, but I have a couple more missions, and then my contract is up."

"We are counting the days, baby. Come home soon," Linda said with pain in her voice.

"You both will be in my arms soon," he said, holding back his tears.

The phone call went silent, and then a little voice said, "I love you, Daddy, don't let the monsters get me and mommy."

Brock Smith held back tears and cleared his throat.

"I won't, baby. Mommy and you are safe forever," he said as a tear rolled down his cheek.

"All Black Fox Company to the airstrip," a voice interrupted over the intercom.

"Okay, my sweetheart, Daddy has to go and get some more monsters. I love you both so very much." As he held the receiver, he started to tear up.

"We love you, Daddy!" a little cheerful voice said over the phone.

"I love you, Brock. Please be safe and come home to us," Linda said with a catch in her throat.

"I love you, Linda. I will be home soon." He hung up the phone, grabbed his pack, and walked out the door, wiping his tears.

***

Sergeant Major Black was loading the CC-177 Globemaster III when he saw Sergeant Smith coming up the strip. Smith's face said it all: he was battered and brokenhearted. Black knew he always called his family before every mission—today, Sergeant Smith's face showed how badly he wanted to retire.

"You ready, brother?" Smith said, wiping his face and adding happiness to his tone.

"Always ready. You?" Black said, staring at his sergeant.

"Yes, yes, I am," Smith smiled as he cocked his pistol and put it into his hip holster.

Corporal Malroy and Master Corporal Santos were already buckled in and set. Black looked around.

"So, we fly to Ottawa, pick up the package, and go?" Malroy asked.

Black looked at Malroy and nodded as he strapped himself in.

"That's the plan, Corporal."

***

The plane lifted off and cruised through the air swiftly and silently. Sergeant Smith had his eyes closed, thinking and picturing his beautiful wife and daughter, missing them every second he had been apart from them.

"You know, before the virus, I was a rock, paper, scissors champion," Malroy said, nudging Santos.

"Impressive," said Smith in a deadpan voice.

"Best out of fifty? We got time," said Malroy, amused by his own comment.

"You really have a lot of time on your hands, eh?" Santos said as he made a fist. "Loser has to clean the winner's gear for a week?"

Corporal Malroy, not even hesitating, made a fist. "You're on."

Meanwhile, Sergeant Major Black sat there, puzzled as to why the President would want to meet with such urgency. Canada and the United States had been closer than ever over the past year; whatever *they* knew Canada would know the second they could call. *A simple phone call would have sufficed,* Black thought. *Must be big; maybe they are losing ground and require assistance.*

Sergeant Smith looked over at the major as Santos and Malroy played rock, paper, scissors.

"What are you thinking, Major?" Smith asked.

"Something isn't right," he said. "To fly us all the way down there for a meeting doesn't make sense. That is a waste of resources and time. It has to be something very big or very secretive. Something that a phone call can't cover."

Whatever it is, I hope we can handle it," Smith said, leaning forward and looking at his boots.

"When have we *not* been able to handle it?" Black said as he leaned back with his eyes closed.

"Just hope it isn't too big, you know? I want to be home with my family," said Smith. "Not out here fighting day in and day out. It's exhausting."

***

About four hours passed, and then the plane started to descend. Sergeant Major Black nodded to the men as they all undid their belts and geared up. All four men stood shoulder to shoulder as the ramp dropped to the ground.

Prime Minister Martin Tremblay stood there with three bodyguards around him. The eyes of the bodyguards impassively took them in.

Black and his team were geared up with combat attire: bulletproof vest, tactical vest, kneepads, and elbow pads as black as a winter's night. Assault rifles rested in all their arms, their pistols strapped to their legs. The Prime Minister's eyes widened as he stared at the most intense, battle-ready bastards he had ever seen.

A man leaned towards the Prime Minister and whispered into his ear, "You want the best, and you got the best. This is the Black Fox Company."

The Prime Minister nodded and walked up to them, shaking their hands.

"Thank you all for coming on such short notice. I feel safer already," the Prime Minister said as he walked past them and went to his seat.

Malroy looked over at Santos and smirked. "He's scared of his own protection," Malroy said under his breath. "He's shaking in his seat,"

Sergeant Major Black looked around and waved Sergeant Smith over to assist him in a walk-around the plane before they took off once again. Black looked at the plane, checking for modifications, as did Sergeant Smith, and both found nothing.

"Let's move out!" Black said, walking back up the ramp as it lifted off the ground.

4. UNITING

"Mr. President, Prime Minister Tremblay is in route now by plane heading for Washington," the secretary said. Her name was Ashley Brooks, and she'd worked with the man since he was a senator.

The President nodded and then rose from his chair, taking a deep breath. "Please get Nova 4 geared up, I want them ready."

A man walked over to the phone and contacted the Washington base. "Get Nova 4 to the White House *now*."

At the base, a man spoke over the intercom: "Nova 4, report to vehicle garage for transport in ten, battle ready."

Sergeant Delmore and Master Corporal Kilghannon dropped their playing cards and looked at each other.

"What happened now?" Delmore said as they rose from their chairs. As Delmore turned to exit the room, Kilghannon flipped his two cards.

"I had you," Kilghannon whispered, looking at Sergeant Delmore's cards.

***

Corporal Ryan Witter and Corporal Rex Witter were already in their bunks getting their battle gear on. Ten minutes later, Nova 4 reported to the garage and got into an armored Humvee.

"Did they breach the borders?" Delmore asked.

The driver shook his head as he kept driving and looking straight.

"Well, what's going on, then?" Ryan Witter asked.

The driver looked into the rear-view mirror. "The President has asked for your team. You will learn the rest when we get you all to the White House," the driver said, looking back at the road and then turning up the White House driveway.

The President's assistant, a man by the name of Muller, was standing on the top step of the stairs that led to the front doors of the White House. Men surrounded him as he stood still, looking at the Humvee. Master Corporal Kilghannon opened his door and stepped out; following him was Corporal Ryan Witter and Corporal Rex Witter. Sergeant Delmore opened his door and slammed it shut. The four men stared at Muller and his men. Silence filled the empty space between the two groups.

"You ordered us here; we are here. What seems to be on everyone's mind?" Sergeant Delmore asked.

"Once Prime Minister Tremblay gets here, we will explain everything," Muller said as he turned his back. "Follow me."

Sergeant Delmore looked at his men and shrugged his shoulders as he started up the White House steps. Kilghannon and the Witter brothers followed Sergeant Delmore up the stairs and through the front doors. Through the main lobby, Nova 4 followed the assistant, passed the Roosevelt Room, and then turned to the right, walking up the stairs to the Cabinet Room where President Gallagher was waiting with two secret service agents.

"Gentlemen, please come in," the President said, standing up.

All the men stood at attention and saluted the commander in chief.

"At ease, gentleman," Gallagher said.

All the men adopted the position of ease and were silent until a woman walked into the room and announced that Prime Minister Tremblay had arrived.

"Bring him here," the President ordered.

Major John Black and Sergeant Brock Smith entered first in full gear.

Black radioed Malroy to bring the Prime Minister in, and a moment later, Santos and Malroy walked in with Prime Minster Martin Tremblay. The President walked over and smiled at the Prime Minister and extended his hand. The Prime Minister smiled back and firmly shook the President's hand.

"How are you, Frank?" the Prime Minister asked.

"Could be better, Martin, as you know, but we need to talk privately first."

"Of course," the prime minster said, looking back at his men and nodding.

All the men flicked the safety switches on their rifles and stepped back at ease. Tremblay and Gallagher walked off through the President's secretary's office, shut the door behind them and continuing into the Oval Office.

***

In the Oval Office, the two leaders sat on the couches facing one another.

"It's China," said the President.

Prime Minister Tremblay let out a slow breath. "China and their nukes. Yes, I thought that might be what this is about. I fear they are going to wipe out the world one country at a time."

"I have an idea," said the President, "but it might seem crazy."

"These days, nothing is crazy anymore."

"We knew long before the outbreak that China had launch-ready short-range nuclear missiles. From our international talks, we all know that China is getting irritated with the infected around their borders and the constant border breaches. I fear they might reach a breaking point and mobilize their short-range nukes and wipe out Mongolia, India, Iran, Kazakhstan, Pakistan, Vietnam, Myanmar, Nepal, Kyrgyzstan, and Japan. Also, if they launch, Russia would be affected by the nukes, and we both know President Volkov will retaliate—and then not only do we have a virus issue, but we will also have a nuclear war that will ultimately end our human race and our fight to survive."

The Prime Minister merely nodded, thinking of the catastrophic issue he had now been faced with.

"If they fire those nukes, everything we have fought so hard to keep will be for nothing," the President explained.

"What do you need from us, Mr. President?" said Prime Minister Tremblay.

"I'm going to keep talking to China's President, but if it comes to the worst-case scenario, I will need the men you came with. Teamed with my four men, they will be the best of the best. We may have a chance to stop this—and, ultimately, keep the fight alive."

President Gallagher shifted forward in his seat. "Look, Martin, I know you need them, but right now the world needs them. If we don't do anything about this, well, then, we might as well sit back and watch the fireworks."

"Of course," said Tremblay. "Take them, and stop this from happening. We have almost regained British Columbia; another couple of weeks, and we can declare it a safe zone. But if the world goes up in nuclear flash, all that work to regain our nation will have been for nothing. Have you tried having a phone call with President Sung?"

"Repeated calls, but no luck in reaching a deal yet. Diplomacy has not been taken off the table with them just yet, and I have high hopes that we can reach some type of agreement. Moscow, at least, has an open line."

Prime Minister Tremblay said, "We must keep the peace in a time like this. I will make calls to Moscow and let them know Canada will support them. Show them we are all one now with one goal."

"Russia is facing hard times; they have been overrun in certain areas. I feel the first mission the team should do is a trip to Moscow. Russia says they have a possible cure, but due to the laboratory being overrun, they no longer have access to it at the moment. President Volkov has given me permission to try and extract the cure from the laboratory. He is currently trying to re-establish his force's bases and the logistics."

"He gave US soldiers permission to operate on Russian soil?" the Prime Minister asked, wide-eyed.

"Yes. So as a trial run, we should send our team to Moscow for the cure, and then if it's retrieved, we can use that as a tool to stop China from nuking everyone. If we don't get it, we go to China and disarm their nukes," the President said, summing up the action plan.

"Disarming their nukes won't be so easy, given the fact that they have mobile units that can fire from anywhere," the Prime Minister said.

"I know, that is why, if we have to go with option two, we will need Russia's help. We have intel that their nukes have satellite-guided tracking systems in each rocket. If we just down the satellites they utilize, then we can temporarily shut them down," said the President.

"Diplomacy is not dead yet," the President said as he stood up. "I will try contacting China again, but if there's no luck. We move forward with this plan."

"You have Canada's support, Mr. President."

"Thank you for your time, and I hope you understand the precautions we took. I can't trust phones anymore; it's better to hear it straight from the mouth these days." The President extended his hand.

The Prime Minister shook the President's. "We will prevail."

Moments passed as the two leaders talked in private; tension built in the room. Sergeant Major Black never once took his eye off Master Corporal Kilghannon, and the same went for Master Corporal Kilghannon, who never blinked as he stared at Sergeant Major Black. All eight men, armed and dangerous, stood in the hallway not knowing what the leaders' conversation consisted of, or what impact it could have on them.

"So . . . you guys selling Girl Guide cookies or something?" Malroy asked.

Kilghannon stepped forward.

"Master Corporal Kilghannon, at ease!" Sergeant Delmore ordered.

"Corporal Malroy . . ." Sergeant Major Black said.

"I'd eat you alive, boy!" Kilghannon said, cracking his neck.

"Well, lucky for you, I shower with seasoning body wash. You like it spicy or mild?" Malroy winked as he chewed his gum.

Sergeant Smith's muscles were bulging as he gripped his weapon, staring at corporals Rex and Ryan Witter, who were staring right back.

After about an hour or so, the door opened, and Prime Minister Tremblay walked out followed by the President Gallagher. A moment of silence fell over the Oval Office, until Ryan Witter spoke up.

"So?"

The President offered for the men to sit, but all declined the gesture.

The President looked at all the men and smiled. "After a long discussion, we have come to a decision, and we are going to proceed with Mission Diplomacy," the President said, then paused.

"Russia," he said, "has had an outbreak within their safe zones and has been temporarily set back, and is therefore requesting help for one thing. Their military was blindsided, and our hearts go out to them, but the point of sending you eight men in is to get a possible cure they have been working on. It is located in a lab on the outskirts of Moscow. The facility is locked down, but infected are all over the place. The drone we flew over several times reads four warm-blooded targets in the facility, possibly human, but as we know, berserkers are warm-blooded."

Sergeant Major Black stepped forward. "So, the mission is to fly to Moscow, rescue the scientist or whoever is in there, and grab the possible cure?"

The Prime Minister stood up. "Yes, Sergeant Major Black, our main focus in life right now is survival. I feel we should take any chance we get at reversing this hell—and so does the President."

Corporal Rex Witter stepped in. "So, we are all teaming up here, sir?"

"We are brother nations, gentlemen," said the President. "We were even before this epidemic, and we will stay together through this. You eight men have been called upon by Canada and the United States of America to fulfill this mission, and if the cure is found, you will be the eight men who saved the human race—the whole world—and we would be indebted to you all." the President said.

All men stood, their minds racing and thinking. Sergeant Smith closed his eyes, picturing his beautiful wife and daughter, thinking of the life they could have if they found the cure and started to change the world back to how it had been before.

Sergeant Smith opened his eyes and stepped forward. "I have fought beside these three men and entrusted my life in their hands. This mission is no different; it is just another mission that we will complete with the help of Nova 4, and we will be successful," Sergeant Smith said, nodding his head to the two leaders.

Sergeant Major Black, Corporal Malroy, and Master Corporal Santos all stepped forward and nodded. Master Corporal Kilghannon and Sergeant Delmore saluted the President and prime minster. Corporal Rex Witter nodded, and then turned to his brother.

Corporal Ryan Witter stood silent for a moment, and then held his head high and smiled. "Let's do it," he said.

The President smiled and clapped his hands, walking around shaking all eight men's hands and saying thank you.

The President looked at all the men, and then at the Prime Minister. "We have picked a name for this group of tough and brave men that I think you will all like," the President said as he pulled out eight patches from his pocket. All eight men looked and read the patch that said "BlackNova 8."

"As the ranking officer, we have selected Sergeant Major Black as the team lead," the President said sternly.

All the men looked at each other; they were the first joint task force since the epidemic started. Master Corporal Santos, Sergeant Smith, Master Corporal Kilghannon, Corporal Malroy, Corporal Ryan Witter, Corporal Rex Witter, Sergeant Delmore, and Sergeant Major Black stood shoulder to shoulder at attention and saluted the world leaders.

"Through hell we fight as one, and as brothers we fight for the greater good of the human race, united by arms. If anyone is left of BlackNova 8, the cure will be returned to the brother countries of Canada and America," Sergeant Major Black said, holding his salute.

After Sergeant Major Black finished, all the men roared, "Hoorah!" The room filled with joy as the men started to talk and get to know one another.

Then the door opened, and the President turned. "Ah yes, Dr. Clase!" he said.

"Sir," Dr. Clase said with a not-so-thrilled tone.

"You shall accompany these men to Moscow to be the American scientist we can trust in the laboratory," the President said, smiling.

Dr. Clase, looking confused as ever, looked around the room with a crooked smile. "Hello, everyone," he said, looking at all the soldiers.

The men all nodded and groaned a greeting to the doctor as he entered the room a little further.

"Okay, well, we have some mission planning to do, so you are all dismissed," the President said.

Sergeant Major Black stepped up quickly. "Sir, actually, if the *team* could do the planning so we are better prepared, and . . . Let's face facts, we have seen more combat then any analyst you can find."

The President and Prime Minister locked eyes for a moment, and then nodded.

"Yes, BlackNova 8, you are responsible for the planning," the President said as he and the Prime Minister exited the room.

A man entered the room and looked at all the soldiers.

"It is getting late, gentleman. Dinner will be served soon. For now, I shall show you to your sleeping quarters," the man said as he turned and walked out of the room.

All the members followed the servant through the White House, down the many corridors and up the stairs until they found themselves in the first room.

"Here are two beds. The rest of the rooms on the left side going that way are all bedrooms for you gentleman," the man said, pointing down the hallway.

"Thank you," Sergeant Delmore said as he picked up his bag and walked down the hallway.

"Me and Master Corporal Santos call dibs!" Malroy said as he ran into a room and jumped on the bed.

"Is he a child or something?" Kilghannon asked Santos.

"You know, I wouldn't doubt it sometimes," Santos chuckled. He picked up his bag and entered the room Malroy had dibbed for them.

5. THE FIRST TIME

THE WHITE HOUSE, WASHINGTON, DC
JUNE 10, 2024 (08:00 HOURS)

The day broke and all the members of BlackNova 8 were rising from their beds. Most the men hadn't had a good sleep in a while. Sergeant Major Black woke from his sleep and looked over at Sergeant Smith, who was sitting up in his bed reading *It* by Stephen King.

"Why do you read these days, Sergeant?" Sergeant Major Black asked as he threw a shirt over his head and let it drop down over his torso.

"Passes the time, brother. Also keeps me calm," Smith said as he put his book down. "I suppose it's time to plan this mission, eh?"

All the men gathered in a private room to look over battle details. The room was concrete and empty except for a long steel table, around which the eight men could discuss the mission. Black leather chairs and bottles of water were provided to the men. Paper covered the table and crumpled balls of paper littered the floor.

"Let's keep it basic, men. This is a rescue-and-grab mission. If all goes well, we won't see any combat, because the facility is locked down," Sergeant Major Black said, standing up from his chair.

"Why can't we just bomb all the infected around the facility and walk right in?" Kilghannon asked.

"A fair question," said Black. "The ground surrounding the facility has sensors so that if it gets bombed, the facility and everything in it is destroyed so no one can have access to their findings or intelligence."

All the men were silent until Corporal Ryan Witter spoke up. "We can't take a helicopter, because it would be too long of a flight—it's already ten hours with a plane—so we either get dropped closer to a point where there is a helicopter, so we could use it to hover over and rappel onto the roof, or we walk right in, guns blazing?"

"We don't want contact with the infected," said Black, "but if need be, it will happen. As for now, we treat this as a stealth mission, so we don't have contact."

"From our understanding, Russia is an ally. We can take the CC-177 Globemaster III over the Atlantic Ocean and land in Moscow; they have an airbase called 'Aerodrom Kubinka' that's five klicks northwest of Moscow Oblast. From there, we are only a twenty-five-minute helicopter flight to Kaluga, where the research lab is located. Once we arrive, the helicopter will drop us onto the roof. From there, we infiltrate the lab with the assistance of Dr. Clase. He will point out the cure, and from there we head back to Aerodrom Kubinka, where we give them the cure and take some for ourselves, as well," Black explained.

"Once I get all the approvals, and Russia agrees with the help, we will be on our way, gentlemen," Sergeant Major Black said as he nodded to the men.

All the men nodded and agreed; then a man came into the room holding a sword. All the men looked nonplussed. The man introduced himself as Jeffery.

"Yeah, Jeff," said Malroy, "I don't think we need swords—we have guns."

"What happens when you run out of ammo? Or your gun jams? Gentlemen, swords have been a man's best friend for ages. They are dependable, they never run out of ammo, they're easy to hide, and if handled right, they can make many victims," Jeffery said.

Jeffery waved his hand as he exited the room, signaling the men to follow.

"What are we, new recruits?" Master Corporal Santos shook his head as they all followed Jeffery.

Jeffery entered a room, followed by BlackNova 8. The room was bare; no windows and only concrete walls surrounded the men. Eight swords lay before the men's feet. The swords were slim and long like katanas with "BlackNova 8" engraved on the handles. All the men reached down and grabbed their swords, taking them out of the sheaths. The men looked amazed.

"They are so light," Malroy said, waving his around.

"Okay, get ready," Jeffery said.

"Ready for what?" Santos asked as a door in the concrete room shifted open slowly.

"What the heck?" Malroy said.

Two infected came running out, blood dripping from their mouths, arms flailing around as they charged the men. All the men dropped their swords, pulled out their pistols, and shot the infected in the head.

Jeffery paused for a moment as the door shut. "Okay, the point of having a sword is not to *drop* it, men," Jeffery said with his head down.

"I'm going to teach you some basics," Jeffery said as he unsheathed his sword and held it in front of him.

Jeffery then swung his sword to the left, then spun, all the while swinging his sword to the right. Then, bending down on one knee, Jeffery switched his wrist and stabbed his sword behind himself. Regaining his stance, Jeffery looked at everyone.

"The key is to keep moving, but always keep an eye on your targets and know where they are," Jeffery explained. "Now, I want you men to hold your swords in front of you, and now slice to the left, and then the right," Jeffery explained.

Hours passed as the men trained and trained. Sweat covered their aching bodies, and their wrists burned with pain from handling their swords. But, they were soldiers, and they fought through the pain and fatigue.

**

The night came quickly, it seemed. A cool breeze hit Sergeant Major Black's face as he stood on the White House's roof, looking down on the city. He allowed his thoughts to wander as he closed his eyes . . .

One of the infected looks over at him, but Black shoots it in the head as he runs by. Corporal Malroy, Sergeant Smith, and Master Corporal Santos then get out of the car and follow him. Bodies are scattered all over the neighborhood, blood turning the grass red. Windows are smashed, and a woman lies dead in Black's driveway, but it's not his wife. He runs into his home, looking around.

"Lisa!" he yells, but there's no answer.

He kicks in his bedroom door and sees the room torn to pieces. Sergeant Smith and Corporal Malroy move downstairs with their rifles raised and their fingers on the trigger. Smith and Malroy turn their scope flashlights on as they search the basement. Santos stands out front to keep a watch out for more infected when he hears the cry of a man whose heart has just been broken.

Santos runs in and sprints up the stairs to find Black on his knees, hovering over his dead wife and daughter, both torn apart violently. Santos is speechless as he stares upon the horror—every soldier's nightmare. Smith and Malroy run up and witness their brother-in-arms crying, holding his dead daughter's hand, and looking at his wife.

Black starts to groan, a deep groan of a battered man. His rage can be felt by everyone in the room. He pounds the floor beneath him as he cries louder and louder. Smith puts his hand on Black's shoulder as a tear runs down Smith's face. Black grabs for his pistol and raises it to his head quickly.

"No!" Sergeant Smith shouts as he smacks the gun out of Black's hand. "You will not die like that, brother!" Smith then gets down on his knees and holds Black in his arms. Malroy and Santos nod to Smith as they go back downstairs to keep guard. Black's grip on Smith's shoulder almost crushes him, but Smith holds him close as he feels his neck become moist from the tears.

"Let's get out of this room, Major. You don't need to see this anymore," Smith says as he helps Black to his feet.

Black steps back. Smith looks in his eyes and sees something worse than the epidemic: the hurt and pain that has filled his eyes instantly. He walks over to his wife and takes the cross necklace from her neck and puts it around his own.

"You are a strong soldier, father, and friend, John. Just remember, they don't have to live in fear every day now, waking up to all this bloody hell," Smith says as he pats Black on the shoulder and leaves the room.

Sergeant Major Black walks over to the flipped dresser and sees a photo of himself with his wife and daughter. He picks the picture up and takes it out of the frame. Rage fills his mind as he looks at the picture. He pockets the picture and runs down the stairs and into the streets. Infected come out from a house across the street and see him.

"Sergeant Major Black, no!" Santos yells as he runs toward him.

The infected charge as Black pulls out his tactical knife. "Come on, you piece of shit!" he says as he runs at the infected. Sergeant Major Black cocks his arm back and drives the knife through the infected's head, along with a part of his hand; the force was just that hard. He pulls the knife out, sees another infected, and runs at it, jump-kicking it in the face. He gets on top of it and stabs the infected repeatedly, each stab filled with more and more rage as the infected's face slowly becomes *mush. He lets out a loud roar as blood covers his face and arms. Santos picks up a small blanket that is in the street and slides over to Black and wipes his face before the blood drips into his eyes or mouth . . .*

"Nice night out here," Sergeant Delmore said as he walked up beside Sergeant Major Black.

Black shook his head to refocus on the present and looked at Sergeant Delmore. "Yeah . . . nice night."

"Listen, I'm not going to stand here and say I'm happy about you being our leader. But rank is to be respected, and I respect the wishes of my commander in chief. I won't give you any issues; I just have to get used to not leading. I have led my men for just over two years now," Sergeant Delmore said, looking over the White House's lawn.

"I appreciate that, Sergeant Delmore," said Black. "I understand we are being relocated to the JB Anacostia-Bolling."

"Yes, my home for the last five years," Delmore said.

"I guess they tease us with the comfy beds for the night and then ship us back to the cold cots we are used to, eh?" Sergeant Major Black joked.

"Seems about right, doesn't it?" Sergeant Delmore laughed.

"Look forward to working together, brother," Delmore said, extending his hand.

"Call me Johnny," Black said as he sternly shook Sergeant Delmore's rough hand.

6. CLOSE COMBAT

Days passed as the gruesome sword training continued, along with the finalization of the battle plan. Morale was high, and the men felt good about the mission. After training one day, Master Corporal Santos and Corporal Malroy went down to the local bar to grab a drink before their mission. The bar was called "One-Shot Wonder." Both Malroy and Santos enjoyed that name as they walked into the bar. They ordered beers and waited at the bar on the barstools.

"How's the family, Master Corporal Santos?" Malroy asked as the bartender handed him his beverage.

"Good. Counting the days—just like Sergeant Smith is—until I can see them," Santos said, sipping his beer.

"I never really asked, but do you have a girlfriend or something?" Santos asked Malroy, laughing.

"No. I did, but she dumped me just before I signed up, and as for family, they gave me up to foster care when I was three, so really, the only family I have is you guys," Malroy said as he sipped his beer.

Master Corporal Santos fell silent for a moment. "Man, well after our duty is done, maybe you'll find that amazing infected girl you've been looking for," Santos said, punching Malroy in the shoulder.

"Master Corporal Santos, how can you stay so calm all the time? That time we were on the roof—you didn't seem fazed at all," said Malroy.

Santos cradled his beer as he stared straight at the wall; then he looked back at the young corporal. "There is a time to be scared, a time to be angry, a time to cry, and a time to act. That was a time to act. Was I scared? Yes. Did I want to run? Yes. I am no Superman; we are all human and get the urge to just run and forget everything. But we have a job, and our job at that moment was to get those survivors to safety," Santos said.

"Guess I still have some learning to do yet," Malroy said.

"You are allowed to be scared, Corporal Malroy," Santos said. "You're just not allowed to show it. We have to be the symbols people run to for safety, hope, and protection. We have a big burden on our shoulders these days. We didn't ask for it, but now we have it, and so we must step up. Without people like us, this world would go to shit, and everything we worked so hard to build would crumble and burn into history," Santos said, exhaling deeply.

"That is deep, man," said Malroy.

"We have fought together a long time, Corporal Malroy. All I am doing is trying to get home to my family. Keep it simple, and we will be fine, brother." Master Corporal Santos smiled.

***

Meanwhile, back at the lab, Dr. Clase was working on getting ready for the mission when he heard a pan fall. He looked over his shoulder.

"Hello?" he called out with a hesitation.

He then went back to packing his tools when he heard a groan. Dr. Clase turned around and saw his assistant standing in the dark.

"Goodness! You startled me, Jack," Dr. Clase said, going back to packing his workbag.

Jack stepped out of the darkness and groaned again.

"Okay, that's enough, Jack," Dr. Clase said, turning around and dropping his bag. "Jack?" Dr. Clase said with fear in his voice.

Jack stood, blood dripping from his mouth, his face all cut up and bloody, teeth sharpened to fangs, eyes turned red. Jack took another step closer. His clothes torn and stained with blood, his body twitching and groaning, Jack stared at Dr. Clase, who slowly backed up toward his desk, pressed the panic button, and set off an alarm.

Jack jerked, and then ran straight at Dr. Clase. He grabbed the doctor and tossed him across the room, slamming him into the wall. Twitching as he picked up Clase, Jack smashed him through a glass door and into the next room, which was filled with blood samples and viruses. Dr. Clase started to crawl—a piece of glass sticking out of his thigh, cuts on his face—toward an incision knife. Jack scratched his own arms until they started to bleed, then picked up a piece of glass and walked toward Dr. Clase.

"Jack, stop, please!" Dr. Clase pleaded.

Jack's eyes widened as he saw the blood leak from Dr. Clase's face and leg. An evil smirk came across Jack's face; he stopped walking and sniffed the air. Jack ran and hid out of sight as two guards came in.

"Dr. Clase?" the guards said as they ran to his aid.

"Watch out!" Dr. Clase yelled.

Jack jumped on the first guard's back and snapped his neck. The cracking sound echoed in the hallway as the guard fell down. The second guard reached for his gun, but Jack stabbed him in the eye with the piece of glass. Blood gushed from his eye as he screamed. Jack pushed the piece of glass further and further, roaring the whole time. The guard started to twitch, and then his body went limp. Jack then took out the piece of glass and started to stab the guards over and over again, blood squirting everyone. Dr. Clase took this moment to grab the incision knife. Jack let out a loud groan as he slid his bloody hands down his face and then turned back to Dr. Clase.

"You are nothing but a no-good berserker!" Dr. Clase said, spitting at Jack's feet.

Jack roared and ran at Dr. Clase. The doctor, with all his strength, sat up off the ground and threw the knife directly into Jack's right eye, killing him instantly. Jack fell hard to the ground, making a loud thud, and blood started to run from his body. Dr. Clase crawled away from the blood trail and pressed the second panic button in the virus room.

Moments later, four guards came and saw the bloody scene. "Oh my god," a guard said, puking off to the side. Two guards ran over to Dr. Clase to help him up.

"I want this place checked. Jack was a berserker, that means one of my specimens is loose or bleeding out," Dr. Clase said as the two guards helped him out of the lab.

"We have an outbreak in the lab!" the one guard said over his radio as he looked around with the other guard.

Dr. Clase was taken to the medical facility beside the lab and dropped off while the other two guards assisted the two that were still in the lab.

***

The phone rang in the Oval Office. The President picked the phone up slowly and then heard the words he wished he would never hear.

"We have a problem in the lab, sir. Dr. Clase was attacked, but he killed the berserker. But still, there is still a concern that the lab is infected, sir."

The President got off his chair and looked at his secretary. "Assemble BlackNova 8, *now*."

Within moments, the entire team was standing on a helicopter pad inside JB Anacostia-Bolling as a UH-60 Black Hawk set down. Five minutes later, they landed on the White House's south lawn. A military man stood on the lawn holding his headdress as the helicopter blades spun around.

Sergeant Major Black jumped out and approached the man, who was a general by the name of Keane.

"We have a problem at USAMRIID. Meet with the guards there, and contain the problem," Keane ordered.

"Yes, sir," Sergeant Major Black said as he quickly ran crouched back to the helicopter. He jumped back into the Black Hawk, and it quickly regained its height and flew toward the USAMRIID.

Moments passed as the men sat looking at each other; this was the first time they would be teaming up as BlackNova 8.

"Thirty seconds," the pilot said over the radio.

Slowly hovering down toward the ground, all the men jumped off and regrouped on the ground around the officer in charge, a colonel named Leeman.

"How many inside, Colonel?" Sergeant Delmore asked as he slipped his gloves on.

"We sent in four guards, but we lost radio contact about nine minutes ago," Leeman replied.

"Understood. Thank you, sir," said Delmore.

"Alright, well, I guess we're up then," Master Corporal Kilghannon said, cocking his assault rifle. All the men were equipped with M4A1 assault rifles with grenade launchers and laser aim scopes.

"Okay, on me, men—when I give the signal to split, Master Corporal Kilghannon, Corporal Rex Witter, Corporal Malroy, and Master Corporal Santos will go one way, Sergeant Smith, Sergeant Delmore, Corporal Ryan Witter, and I will go the opposite. We need to cover as much ground as possible to weed out the infected before they break out," Sergeant Major Black ordered as he started to walk toward the building.

Sergeant Major Black pushed the door slowly open and entered. Everyone followed in a line until they were all in and dispersed around to check the area. Black pointed at Malroy and Ryan

Witter to check the rooms on the left side of the hallway, and then he pointed at Smith and Kilghannon to check the rooms on the right. Black, Delmore, Rex Witter, and Santos continued down the hallway to the end, then stopped and looked down the two hallways leading away from one another.

Smith, Malroy, Ryan Witter, and Kilghannon cleared all the rooms and pressed forward to meet up with the others. Black gave the signal, and Kilghannon, Rex Witter, Malroy, and Santos nodded and broke off to the left while the rest went right. A foul smell came from down the hallway Black and his team went down, then a grunt was heard, Black waved to the ground, signaling everyone to crouch. Black crept to the edge of the wall and peered around the corner to see two guards eating the organs of the other two guards, ripping them apart piece by piece. Black backed up, held up two fingers, and then tapped the handle of his sword. Santos and Delmore withdrew their swords and moved past Black, creeping around the corner.

Santos and Delmore raised their weapons, and at just the last second, the infected looked back as two blades cut through the foul air. Two heads rolled out in the open as Black and Rex Witter stood up and moved forward. Black went over the radio and whispered, "Two down, now finishing off the guards so no more infected rise."

***

Meanwhile Sergeant Smith pushed open a door and entered a room followed by Ryan Witter, Malroy, and Kilghannon. The sound of glass being crunched underfoot rumbled in the men's eardrums as they turned to see a woman twitching uncontrollably, staring at them and licking glass that was covered in blood.

"That's not right," Malroy whispered.

The woman walked out in the open and was missing a chunk of her hip and arm. She was covered in blood, her cheeks had holes in them, and her jaw sagged as if it were dislocated. Malroy pulled out his sword and slowly stepped in front of everyone. The woman groaned as she moved closer and closer. Malroy raised his blade, and with a strong strike, sliced the women's head off with such force that it flew through the air and smashed a glass shelf. Black and his squad heard it and then instantly heard groans from down the hall.

"They know we are here, I repeat, they know we are here! No more swords!" Black ordered as he cocked his M4A1 assault rifle and stood up from his crouched position to see two infected charging. Black shot both in the head and continued forward. Delmore and Santos switched places so that their backs were to Black and Rex Witter as they moved forward down the hall.

Then, over the radio, came a voice. "BlackNova 8, the staff list says there are seven people excluding Dr. Clase working today," Radio tech Mark warned the team.

"Copy that. I have killed two workers so far," Black said.

"I killed one," Corporal Malroy said over the radio

"So, that means there are still four workers. What happened to the guards?" he asked.

"All dead," Black said.

Sergeant Major Black and his squad moved into what almost looked like a jail. Animals in cages roared and pounded against the cage bars.

"What did they do here?" Rex Witter said as he looked around.

Delmore and Ryan Witter stopped and saw the three specimens that they had helped Dr. Clase obtain.

"Hey, Sergeant Major Black, come here," Delmore said.

Black walked over to the sergeant. "What's up?" Black asked.

"Before we met, my team helped Dr. Clase get these three specimens for human trials, but they are still locked up and their mouths are wired shut."

"I'm not following you, Sergeant."

"So, if their mouths are still wired shut, how did this infection break out?"

"Good find. Keep that intel with you until we get out, and we will find answers," Black said.

Then a bang at the door boomed through the room. All four men pointed their weapons at the door for a moment. Then Black ordered Rex Witter to open the door. Witter waited until Black gave him the nod.

Rex Witter quickly opened the door, and a Chinese scientist came out, yelling, "Don't shoot! I'm human! Don't shoot!"

"Hold your fire," Sergeant Major Black ordered as the man scrambled to his feet.

"We have to get out of here! Help me, they are everywhere!" the man said frantically.

"Be quiet!" Black ordered, but the man kept yelling and screaming until Sergeant Delmore grabbed the scientist and punched him in the face, knocking him out.

"Sorry, but he was getting annoying," Delmore said.

"Annoying, yes, but it's just like 'you smelt it you dealt it': you knock them out, you carry them out," Black said as he started to walk out of the room.

Rex Witter and Santos laughed as they helped get the scientist onto Delmore's back.

"We have a survivor," Black said over the radio.

"We killed the last three workers, so I'm assuming the person you have is number four," Malroy said.

"Regroup outside the front doors," Black said over the radio.

Moments later, all eight men were outside with the scientist, who was slowly regaining consciousness.

Black spoke to Colonel Leeman. "Your building is clear. Bring in the cleanup team to disinfect everything, and to get rid of the bodies so the infection doesn't spread. We got lucky today."

The scientist got off Delmore's shoulders and looked around. "We need to question you, sir," the sergeant said as he led the scientist to a Humvee.

"Sir, we are bringing the survivor to the medical wing of the JB Anacostia-Bolling to be treated," Malroy said over the radio.

"You got a name there, buddy?" Kilghannon asked.

"My . . . my name is Young, Young Sue," he said.

***

The Humvees, after a thirty-minute drive down Route 270, turned onto the 495 and then pulled up to the medical wing doors. Kilghannon and Rex Witter helped Dr. Sue out of the Humvee and walked him to the medical wing. Black and Smith drove the Humvees over to the garage and parked them. Two soldiers walked over with gas pumps to fill the Humvees up.

"I could get used to *this*," Malroy said, walking behind Black and Smith. Dr. Sue was escorted by two nurses to a room for examination.

"Any word on Dr. Clase?" Black radioed.

"Dr. Clase is going to be fine, no wounds or infection detected. He's in recovery. He will be fine," a voice responded over the radio.

"Copy that," Black answered.

***

Later that day, after everything settled down, Master Corporal Santos and Corporal Ryan Witter went to the medical wing to see Dr. Sue.

"Hello, we are here to question Dr. Sue about the events that took place today," Corporal Witter said.

"Oh, he was discharged about two hours after you men dropped him off," a nurse said.

"What?" Witter said, stunned at the news he had just heard.

Santos stepped in and asked, "By whose authority?"

The nurse paused and looked through her notes. "A man by the name of Dr. Clase."

"Why would Dr. Clase discharge Dr. Sue?" Witter asked.

Santos paused for a minute, and then walked out of the medical wing. "I need a location on Dr. Clase ASAP!" Santos ordered.

"Is he not still in the medical wing at the JB Anacostia-Bolling?" a voice said over the radio.

"No!" Master Corporal Santos exclaimed over the radio.

Sergeant Smith picked up his radio after hearing Santos' troubled voice. "What happened?"

"Dr. Clase and Dr. Sue are missing, and they are the only two survivors of the outbreak at USAMRIID," Santos said.

"We will find them. They couldn't have gone far, I'm sure," Smith said. "Sergeant Major Black?"

Black looked at Smith for a moment before speaking. "I think Dr. Clase and Dr. Sue did something in that lab that caused all this."

"I feel the same way," Smith said.

Walking out of the White House, Black found two soldiers.

"Hey, I need three scout teams to roam the area looking for the two missing doctors," Black ordered.

Both soldiers saluted, threw their cigarettes away, and ran to their vehicles to go gather more men.

"Sergeant Major Black to JB Anacostia-Bolling control. I am sending out patrols to locate Dr. Clase and Dr. Sue."

"Control to Sergeant Major Black, copy that."

Sergeant Major Black walked into the intelligence room where both the base and the White House was being monitored and kept safe. Black saw Santos sitting down, looking over files.

"Andy," Black said, sitting down.

"Hey, any word on if we found Dr. Clase?" Santos asked.

"Scout teams came up blank; he just disappeared," Black said, shaking his head in disbelief. "Find anything?"

"Everything looks normal, although there is one test tube in his lab labeled 'Oval,' and that seems a bit worrisome, and I am looking further into it," Santos said as he turned a page.

"Alright, well I'll leave you to it, Master Corporal," Black said, patting Santos on the back and leaving the room.

***

Meanwhile, in the training room, Sergeant Delmore and Corporal Rex Witter were working out.

"Come on, one more," Corporal Rex Witter said, spotting Sergeant Delmore as he benched 225 pounds.

Sergeant Delmore exhaled heavily and pushed the weight back into the racks.

"You're getting old, eh?" Corporal Rex Witter laughed as Sergeant Delmore got to his feet.

"I can still kick your ass, kid," Sergeant Delmore chuckled.

Corporal Rex Witter got into position and started lifting the weight that Sergeant Delmore had been using. Corporal Rex Witter smiled as he stared at Sergeant Delmore, not seeming to be phased by the weight at all.

"Ah, whatever, youngster," Sergeant Delmore said as he tossed his towel at him.

"Not going to spot me?" Corporal Rex Witter laughed.

"I hope the bar crushes your skull—not that there's much in there," Sergeant Delmore laughed as he walked toward the showers.

Meanwhile, in Corporal Malroy's room, Malroy lay in his bed peacefully and quiet with his eyes closed.

"You got my six," Waters said.

Malroy shot up from his dead sleep and looked around his room in a panic. Sweat covered his body, and he had to slow his breathing. He changed positions on his bed and was now sitting on the edge, staring at the ground, his hand trembling as he stared at it.

"I should have had your six, Brian," Malroy said to himself as a tear ran down his face.

Malroy made a fist and punched his bed, then punched it again, rage starting to build as he got to his feet and tossed his pillows, then walked over to his dresser and shook it viciously. He took a deep breath and held it for a moment; he could feel the anger begin to leave his body as he slowly exhaled. Ryan Witter spoke up as he watched Malroy relieve his own stress.

"We are all here for each other, Corporal Malroy—no one knows our pain but each other. You think these world leaders know what it's like to kill a man, or an infected? Do you think they know what it's like to walk into a dark room knowing there are infected somewhere waiting to eat us? No one knows what we do or how we do it, but we always find a way to get through the day. We need to lean on each other," Witter said. He put his hand on Malroy's shoulder. "Everyone depends on us to save the day, and we depend on each other to just get home safe."

Malroy nodded. "You sound like Master Corporal Santos."

"I had a breakdown a couple of days ago, Corporal Malroy, and Master Corporal Santos was there for me as I am here for you," Witter said. "Master Corporal Santos is actually pretty smart."

"Yeah, he's like Yoda," said Malroy.

Witter smiled. "Yeah, I can see that."

Malroy took a deep breath.

Witter said, "Try going for a run or something sometime; I find that helps."

***

The next day came, and all the men reported to the mission room. Sergeant Major Black walked in with a whiteboard and set it up.

"Okay, we got the clearances required to take the CC-177 Globemaster III over the Atlantic Ocean and land in Moscow;

the airbase Aerodrom Kubinka is five klicks northwest of Moscow Oblast. From there, we are only a twenty-five-minute helicopter flight to Kaluga, where the research lab is located. Once we arrive, the helicopter will drop us onto the roof, and from there we infiltrate the lab. Given the Dr. Clase issue, we have asked Russia to supply a scientist who not only knows where things are but can read Russian. He will point out the cure, and from there, we head back to Aerodrom Kubinka, where we give them the cure and take some for ourselves, as well.

All the men nodded.

"Let's get 'em boys," Black said.

"Hoorah!" the men roared as they all stood and went to get geared up.

"Wheels up in thirty, tell the wives you'll be home by dinner tomorrow," Black finished.

All the men gathered in the locker room, gearing up their weapons and protection. Black pulled his gloves over his hands when Kilghannon looked over.

"Something wrong with your knuckles, buddy?" Kilghannon asked.

Sergeant Major Black chuckled. "Nope, just a little modification I made," Black said, pointing to his knuckles. "Steel spikes in my knuckles for punching," he smirked.

Kilghannon looked at Sergeant Major Black in amazement. "You are one scary cat," he laughed as he slapped Black's back.

BlackNova 8 assembled in the garage and stood at attention when the President came in.

"At ease, men," the President paused. "Now, listen up. You men have been chosen because you are the best at what you do: killing and getting the job done. I don't have to tell you how important this is. If the cure is found, then we can reverse this hell that has rained down upon us. Remember what you are fighting for, remember who you are fighting with, and with that, I wish you all luck. I will personally be praying for all of you." The President nodded to the men, and then exited the base garage and went back to his convoy of three black Suburbans.

7. RUSSIA

All the men were strapped in their seats while the CC-177 Globemaster III sat on the runway of the JB Anacostia-Bolling airbase. The Globemaster was vast on the inside; rows of empty seats sat behind BlackNova 8. The men somewhat spread out from each other to give each other space for the long flight ahead of them to Moscow Oblast Airport. When they arrived, three armored Humvees were to be waiting on the landing strip to take them directly to Aerodrom Kubinka.

Malroy looked around the CC-177 Globemaster III, and all the memories of him in the Middle East and coming home came to mind. His first plane ride to a different country was on a Globemaster. Now that he thought about it, every time he went overseas he was taken there on a Globemaster.

I guess some things never change, he thought.

"All clear for takeoff," the captain said over the speaker.

There were two satellite phones supplied to them so they could call their loved ones. Santos was the first to use it.

They all looked ready to kill or be killed. Black saw Smith reading a letter. Sergeant Smith always gave the letter to him at the beginning of missions, but this time he didn't. Smith finished reading the letter, slid it into his back pocket, and then rested his head on the backrest.

"Not giving it to me this time, brother?" Black asked.

"Not this time—I'm feeling good about this one," Smith cracked a smile.

Sergeant Major Black nodded. "Love the attitude."

Malroy walked over to Kilghannon holding onto handgrips as he took his seat. "So, I want to apologize," Malroy said. "It's not that I thought you were *actually* selling Girl Guide cookies that day. It's just, I was really craving those mint ones, and so I lashed out." Malroy's face didn't betray even a *hint* of a smile.

"You are the joker, aren't you?" Kilghannon laughed, pushing Malroy.

Santos was on the laptop looking over the files on Dr. Clase when he found one that was password-locked. "Hey, Sergeant Major Black, I got a document that is password protected. I think it's what we have been looking for."

Black came and sat next to Santos and looked at the screen. "We will have to get some tech guy to see if he can unlock it for us. Good find, Master Corporal Santos."

The Witter brothers sat with their eyes closed and heads back against the headrest.

"So, me and Jennifer did some stuff last night," Ryan said.

"You know, bro, I simply do not care," Rex said.

"Oh, it was nasty, bro," said Ryan. "Mind you, she's played before."

Rex opened his eyes and looked at his brother. "Okay, what are you talking about?"

"Oh, *now* you care?" Ryan laughed.

Rex laughed as he returned to his sleeping position. "You know what? No. I still don't care."

Malroy sat next to Santos, looking entirely guilty of something. "Hey."

Santos peered over at him. "What did you do?"

"I farted next to Kilghannon, and now I'm over here waiting for the bomb to reach his nose, be cool," Malroy said calmly, watching Kilghannon.

"Sometimes I wonder about you, Corporal Malroy," Santos said, returning to the laptop.

"Hey, someone has to lighten the mood, we could all die in a couple hours," Malroy said, his eyes still on his intended victim.

"So, you thought Master Corporal Kilghannon would like to smell shit before he died?" Santos said sarcastically.

Corporal Malroy held back his laugh. "Oh, that's so true."

"Who the hell farted!" Kilghannon exclaimed, looking at everyone.

"He's going to kick your ass," Santos said calmly.

"You'll get yours, prankster," Kilghannon said, sitting back down.

"Oh, come on, it was funny!" Malroy replied.

***

Sergeant Delmore was looking out the window. The night sky was so dark it was almost relaxing; it was as if the world below didn't exist, and for a moment, he loved the feeling of calm and peace. Black walked over and sat next to him, now looking out the window as well.

"Beautiful isn't it," Delmore said softly.

Black paused as he took in the darkness. "Very."

Near the end of the flight, all the men became quiet, most thinking about home. Thoughts of not returning to America could not be avoided, or the fact that death was staring them in the face once again. They all knew the joke about cheating death—which was something all of them had previously done. But for some, it felt like they could cheat it one more time. They didn't want to get hopeful, because it would set them up for utter disappointment if the cure were not found—but they also needed to focus. Now was not the time to look into the future; it was time to focus their minds and mentally prepare.

The team had started to come together, almost like a family. They began to understand each other, their behaviors, likes and dislikes. They had all realized that the fate of the world rested on their shoulders. Although the weight of the world was heavy, they knew that if they all held their own and together fought as one, the weight wouldn't seem so heavy. Their first mission to Russia would not only be a test of chemistry within the team, but it also could be the only mission they would ever do together. If the cure were to be found, just as soon as they came together, they would disband; for some, this meant they could go home and live some type of a normal life. For others, it meant the end of everything they knew.

"Five minutes from the drop point," the pilot said over the intercom.

***

Back at the White House, President Gallagher tried calling Russia. After a couple tries, President Vadim Volkov came on the line.

"Vadim, BlackNova 8 is inbound, about forty-five minutes out. I wanted to call and personally say I appreciate the cooperation."

"My pleasure, Mr. President, I have my military waiting for them now. The scientist I have chosen is a good man, dedicated to science."

"Good, glad to hear it," Gallagher said. "May God be with you, hopefully the next call we have is one worthy of celebration."

"Thank you, Mr. President, I hope the same. Goodbye, Frank," Volkov said as he hung up the phone.

"Goodbye," said President Gallagher

***

Back in the Globemaster III, the green light flicked on, and the pilot came over the PA system: "One minute to Moscow Oblast."

Everyone got up and readied themselves. Loading up their packs and weapons, all the men grabbed the strap handles as the Globemaster made contact with the runway. Once it came to a halt, the rear loading ramp began to slowly descend to the ground. Russian special forces soldiers began to come into view of BlackNova 8, standing fully geared in front of four armored Humvees with fifty-caliber machine guns attached to the tops. The black paint job gave the Humvees a sinister look.

BlackNova 8 exited the Globemaster, and Sergeant Major Black walked up to the man standing slightly in front of his men. The airport was abandoned and clearly under strict military control; there were guards stationed in the towers and chained fences built around the parts that were still standing. It was obvious they had worked hard to take back the Moscow airport.

"Hello, I am Major John Black with BlackNova 8, coming from the US." Sergeant Major Black extended his hand.

"Da, I am Captain Vitaly Petrov," he shook Black's hand, "and this is my second in command, Yuri Sokolov, and as requested, the scientist Vasily Popov."

"Thank you for your assistance in this matter, Captain Petrov," Black said.

"Whatever it takes to get our Motherland back to her glory," Petrov said.

"Please, load up. We are leaving now," Petrov said bluntly.

BlackNova 8 loaded up into the Humvees with the Russian and began their drive to Aerodrom Kubinka. The drive was almost refreshing for BlackNova 8; the vast lands of Russia looked almost untouched. Green grasslands stretched for miles and miles, it seemed. Master Corporal stuck his face out the Humvee's window, and for once he smelt fresh, warm air. It was a moment of pure bliss for him.

"So, the infected have become a nuisance, I hear," Kilghannon said.

"Yes, problem. But we fix," Petrov answered.

"We are nearing our base. We ask you to put on these headscarves until inside. Although we are friendly now, we cannot guarantee you won't attack once everything is settled," Captain Petrov ordered.

Black stared at Petrov with stone-cold eyes. No one knew what Black was going to say. Captain Petrov stopped the convoy and handed out the headscarves.

"No funny business," Black said as he slowly put on the headscarf, which completely shut out his vision of the outside world.

A couple of turns and bumps later, they removed their headscarves and saw themselves in the middle of a runway.

"The helicopter that will take you to laboratory is over there," Petrov said, pointing.

"Thanks for the lift," Black said as he began to exit the Humvee.

Vasily Popov exited his Humvee and gripped his briefcase with a tense grip. Petrov began to speak Russian to Vasily, and he put his hand on his shoulder.

"I don't like this, sir," Malroy stated quietly.

"Stay close . . . everyone," Black instructed.

"Please board the Kamov Ka-29, right over there," Petrov ordered.

BlackNova 8 all gathered into the Kamov Ka-29, followed by Dr. Popov.

"It is a twenty-two-minute flight to Kaluga. From there, you will descend by the rope ladders located above your heads on each side. The pilot will hover nearby until you call in extraction. Once he hears that, he will pick you all up. Good luck," Petrov said as he slammed the helicopter door and gave the thumbs up.

The Kamov Ka-29 slowly began to take off, and once again, BlackNova 8 was in the air on their way to the laboratory in Kaluga. The men began mentality preparing themselves. This was the moment they had done all the planning for. So far, so good—they had positive signs that the mission would go well.

"You know what you have to do?" Smith asked Dr. Popov.

"Yes . . . yes, I do," Popov stuttered.

"Scared?" Sergeant Smith asked.

"I have never seen infected outside of a laboratory," Popov said.

"Don't worry, Doc. We have your back," Smith said.

Moments later, the laboratory came into view, so Black turned around and faced everyone.

"The first person down will guard the ladders until we are all down," Black said as the pilot started to hover over the roof. "Sergeant Smith, you are on Dr. Popov the *entire* time."

"Yes, sir," Smith answered.

"Gas masks on, silencers attached!" Black commanded.

All the men pulled on their gas mask and screwed on their silencers. Sergeant Smith helped Dr. Popov with his gas mask. The pilot got the Kamov Ka-29 right over the roof of the laboratory and gave the thumbs up.

"Go, go, go!" Black roared.

Kilghannon and Delmore hit the roof first. Turning their backs to the rope ladders, they waited as Witters came down. They were followed by Malroy and Santos, Smith and Dr. Popov, and finally Black.

Malroy looked over the edge and saw infected everywhere around the laboratory. *Holy shit*, he thought.

"Let's move. Witters, you two stay up top and keep this roof clear," commanded Black. "The rest on me."

Black tried the roof access door, but it was locked. He signaled Malroy to turn around, dispatching the charges from his pack and placing them on the locked door.

"Fire in the hole," Black roared as the door blasted into pieces.

Malroy and Santos entered first down the stairwell. Once they reached the bottom, they took a kneeling position, their backs facing each other as they peered both ways down the glossy red-floored hallways. Kilghannon and Delmore followed and relieved Santos and Malroy of their position so they could move forward to the ends of the hall, now leaning up against the walls and peering around the corners.

Smith and Dr. Popov walked down the stairs, followed by Black.

"Sergeant Smith, Dr. Popov, and myself will go on and find Room 1936A. Sergeant Delmore and Master Corporal Kilghannon, station yourselves here and keep this area clear," Black ordered.

Dr. Popov gestured towards the sign reading "Room 1900A–1945A," which was pointing in the direction Malroy was stationed.

"That's good, let's move," Black said.

They moved swiftly through the hall and passed Malroy, Smith walking ahead and Black a few steps behind with Dr. Popov. They needed to ensure Popov's safety, or the mission would fall apart.

Dr. Popov whispered, "Three doors down, on the left."

Smith ran up to the door and pressed himself up against the wall, slowly peering into the room.

"Two infected," Smith reported.

"Eliminate," Black ordered.

Smith slowly opened the door and shot two perfect rounds, one for each infected head. He quickly surveyed the room and gave the thumbs up. Black and Popov moved into the room and shut the door behind them.

"Okay, Dr. Popov," Black said. "Find us the cure so we can get out of here."

Popov began looking through vials, one rack at a time.

"How we are doing up top?" Black asked.

"All good, sir. Kind of feels like we are at a concert and we are the superstars, though. Lots of infected down there," Ryan Witter reported.

"That's about as close as you'll get to fame, my friend," Black joked.

Back at the stairwell, Santos snapped his fingers. "Three infected moving down my hallway," he reported.

"Eliminate them," Black ordered as he watched Dr. Popov rummaging through the drawers.

Santos took aim and dispatched the infected. "Infected down, hallway clear," he reported.

Everything seemed to be going smoothly, when suddenly, the sound of smashing glass echoed in the hallways.

"Do we have eyes on what made that sound?" Black asked.

"I don't see anything, sir," Malroy reported.

"Me neither," Santos reported.

"Hey, guys, I think the infected are getting into the building!" Rex Witter reported as he saw hundreds of infected filling into the broken window.

"Shit, Dr. Popov, anything?" Sergeant Major Black asked.

"I look, I look," Popov shouted.

"Corporal Witter, what window broke? Black asked.

"North side, north side!" Ryan Witter reported.

"Corporal Malroy, abandon your post and go to the north side with Santos. Protect that stairwell!" Black ordered.

"Yes, sir," Malroy said as he got to his feet and ran down the hallway.

Groans could be heard echoing in the halls now; gurgling and other fluid-like sounds came closer and closer until the first infected appeared from around the corner.

"Infected, north side, horde!" Santos reported as he began to lay fire on the horde.

Delmore and Kilghannon ran to the north hallway and began firing alongside Malroy and Santos.

"Controlled burst, two shooting at a time," Delmore instructed.

Malroy and Santos, on one knee, systematically began short bursts of fire, eliminating infected after infected.

"Out!" Malroy yelled as he discarded his empty magazine on the floor and reached for another one. Delmore and Kilghannon stepped in front and began firing on the horde.

"Sir, Corporal Ryan Witter is coming down for support," Rex Witter reported.

Ryan Witter made it to the bottom of the stairs when suddenly he was knocked off his feet by something solid. He quickly turned on his back and saw a berserker coming for him again. He quickly got to his feet and was about to pull out his sidearm when the berserker tackled him through the glass wall and into another room.

Through the chaos, Ryan didn't lose track of the berserker, who never stopped attacking. The old-scientist-turned-berserker went for his gas mask, but Ryan grabbed his wrist, and in one fluid motion, placed his feet on the berserker's stomach as he was about to pounce, and then kicked him off and away from himself. Quickly getting to his feet just as the berserker got to his own feet and charged, Ryan pulled his sidearm and shot the berserker directly through its left eye socket, killing it instantly. Ryan took a deep breath and re-holstered him sidearm, running back to his rifle and joining his comrades in the north hallway.

Dr. Popov opened drawer after drawer; then he began pulling the drawers right out in a fit of rage.

"Dr. Popov, look at me and focus. You have to think; they were just working on it when the infected broke out in here. Where would it be?" Smith said softly.

Dr. Popov's eyes widened as he ran past Smith and looked through a microscope.

"Here! But it's only a small sample. We have more. This will not be enough," Dr. Vasily claimed.

"Keep looking," Black demanded.

"Sir, did we request an extraction? We have a chopper inbound," Rex Witter reported from the roof.

"What? No," Black replied.

"We may have company then, sir," Witter said as he watched the chopper come closer.

Once he got close enough, bullets started to hit the roof around the corporal.

"Hostiles! Hostiles on the roof, incoming," Witter said as he took cover behind the cement covering of the roof access.

Sergeant Major Black paused for a moment; there were infected in the north hallway, the sample had been found but it was not enough, and there were hostiles on the roof.

We need a clean exit.

"Dr. Popov, Secure the sample now! We are moving," Black ordered.

Popov quickly grabbed the sample and put it into a vial, then opened his briefcase and secured it.

"North hallway team, we are moving. Start your way toward the stairwell. Corporal Rex, begin defensive maneuvers, we are coming up," Black ordered sternly.

Black and Smith ran down the hallway with Dr. Popov and his briefcase when they saw everyone else firing into a horde of infected.

"Sergeant Delmore and Sergeant Smith, take Dr. Popov to the roof *now*," Black ordered.

"Corporal Rex, we got three coming up. Cover the door so they can make a break for the dip in the roof to provide them cover," Black ordered as he took up a position in the line and began firing on the infected.

"We need an evacuation *now!*" Ryan Witter ordered.

"Evacuation in two minutes," the Russian pilot answered.

"This is going to be a hot extraction, I repeat, hot extraction," Black roared.

"Fall back!" Black ordered as he pulled out two grenades.

Everyone began to back up toward the stairwell as Black pulled the pins on the grenades and tossed them far back into the horde. Five seconds later, an explosion filled the building, just as they took cover in the stairwell.

"Move, move, move," Black said.

Kilghannon and Malroy began firing at the few remaining infected, as another wave of the horde was surely coming.

"I'm running low, sir," Malroy reported.

Black tossed Malroy the rest of his magazines.

"Santos and Malroy, hold this stairwell, split those between you guys. When I give the order, hall ass up the stairs—there will be a chopper waiting," Black ordered.

"Yes, sir!" both men roared as they took up their positions halfway up the stairwell, creating a kill zone for the infected to enter.

Black, Ryan, and Kilghannon began up the stairs and entered into the firefight.

"Sir, the Chinese are here," Rex Witter reported.

Two Chinese soldiers advanced toward their position, but they were quickly gunned down.

"Push forward, men!" Black ordered.

All the men took five steps forward and found new cover, continuing their fire on the Chinese. A Chinese soldier shouted something loud; no one understood it until Delmore saw a grenade land beside him, Dr. Popov, and Smith.

"Nope!" Delmore yelled as he quickly tossed the grenade away, causing it to blow up in the air and not beside him and his comrades.

Smith shot another Chinese soldier, causing them to fall back. Their helicopter came back and dropped ladders.

"Let them retreat—we cannot have two fronts going," Black ordered.

Major looked over and saw their Kamov Ka-29 chopper closing in.

"Santos, Malroy, get out of there, now!" Black ordered.

Santos and Malroy fired a couple more rounds and then began sprinting up the stairs as the infected charged after them.

The Russian pilot hovered as the copilot dropped the rope ladders down. Everyone began climbing up as quickly as possible.

Black and Kilghannon provided cover as Santos and Malroy came running out of the stairwell with infected close behind. Black and Kilghannon began shooting as soon as the first infected emerged onto the roof.

The last Chinese soldier was on the rope ladder leading to the Chinese helicopter when he turned and saw Black shooting the infected. He pulled out his sidearm and aimed at Black, firing a couple rounds as he took off.

Black heard a kind of *zip* sound and began to feel immense pain coming from his left stomach area.

"Ugh!" Black roared as he fell to one knee, holding his stomach as blood began to ooze out.

"Major is hit!" Kilghannon said as he slung his rifle on his shoulder and began to help Black, who was in terrible pain.

"Sorry, sir. This is going to hurt," he yelled as he picked up Black, slung him over his shoulder, and carried him to the ropes.

"Cover them!" Delmore roared as they all began to fire on the infected from the helicopter.

"Up, up, up!" Santos yelled, as he and Malroy were running out of roof.

Just as they got to the ledge, Santos and Malroy jumped and each grabbed a rope ladder, and the helicopter got away from the now-swarmed rooftop.

"Hang on, Eddie!" Smith roared as they began to hastily pull up the rope ladders.

"I got him, I won't let go!" Kilghannon roared as Black ached in terrible pain.

Warm blood trickled down Kilghannon's neck as the chopper flew through the air.

"Get him in!" Smith ordered.

Kilghannon shrugged his shoulders, raising Sergeant Major Black higher so that Santos and Smith could grab him.

"Sergeant Major Black, look at me buddy, come on!" Santos said as he applied pressure to Black's wound.

"We need to get back to the base, now!" Santos demanded.

"We will be there in fifteen minutes," the Russian pilot said.

"Kamov Ka-29 to Kubinka, we have one shot, requesting medical personnel waiting at landing pad, one shot to the abdomen."

Master Corporal Santos pulled out a bandage and applied pressure to Sergeant Major Black's stomach.

"Sergeant Smith, get the tweezers from my back pocket, we need the bullet out now!" Santos demanded.

Smith grabbed the tweezers and handed them to Santos. Smith then grabbed some water and cleaned the wound as Santos dug in. Black rose quickly as the pain took him out of his unconscious state. Black roared and pushed Santos back. Smith grabbed Black's shoulders and pressed him against the ground of the helicopter.

"Stay down, Sergeant Major Black," Smith yelled, holding Sergeant Major Black down.

"Flip him over," Santos said. "It might be a through and through wound."

Smith managed to contain Black and turned him very slightly as Black roared in pain.

"It went through. Just apply pressure to both ends," Santos said, handing Smith more bandages.

"Sergeant Major Black, just breathe, man—stay still," Smith yelled as he pushed hard on Black's wound.

"Medical staff is waiting at the landing pad," the Russian pilot said as the base came into view.

The Kamov Ka-29 barely touched down when the medical staff grabbed Sergeant Major Black and secured him on a stretcher. The doctors and nurses began yelling in Russian as they took Black away toward the medical wing for surgery.

All BlackNova 8 could do was wait and hope for the best for their friend.

8. TIME

Sergeant Smith paced back and forth as he watched the clock. His best friend lay on a surgical table, fighting for his life.

"Sergeant Smith," Captain Petrov said.

"Yes," Smith replied, turning to Petrov.

"I understand there was an issue—how is he doing?" Petrov asked, no concern in his voice.

"I am not sure, he was bleeding a lot in the helicopter. We tried our best to slow it down."

"We have the best doctors here," said Petrov. "I'm sure he will be okay, Sergeant Smith."

"Do you know how the Chinese found out about the mission?" Smith asked with a stern tone.

"What are you implying, Sergeant Smith?"

"You know *exactly* what I'm asking," Smith said, now face to face with the Russian Captain.

"You better watch your tone, Sergeant. Remember where you are standing. This is Mother Russia, not America," Petrov said as he slowly turned and walked down the hall toward the exit.

President Volkov came into the medical wing, greeting Sergeant Smith.

"Hello, Sergeant Smith, my condolences for your friend. I wish him a speedy recovery," President Volkov said, shaking Sergeant Smith's hand.

"Thank you, sir," Smith said with a cold tone.

"I must place a phone call to President Gallagher now, but I wanted to thank you for retrieving the cure for us. Hopefully this mess will soon be cleaned up, and you all can go home as heroes," President Volkov said as he turned and walked away.

***

President Volkov walked into his office and shut the door behind him.

"Please get me the President Gallagher on the phone," he said in Russian to his secretary.

Moments later, President Volkov was greeted.

"President Volkov, I hear we got it," Gallagher said happily.

"Yes, yes we did. But we only retrieved a small amount, unfortunately. Until we can make a bigger dose for your scientist to work with, we will have to keep it here so we don't risk the chance of losing it. You understand—right, Mr. President?" President Volkov said.

"That makes sense," Gallagher said. "When will we break the news to China?"

"Once we have some of the cure made to bring to the table. The Chinese won't believe anything we say without results at this point," President Volkov said.

"We should at least hint to them that we have something. I heard they showed up at your lab, as well," Gallagher said. "How did they find out, President Volkov?"

"It's politics, Mr. President. I told both of you about the cure so there would be no animosity."

Sitting in the Oval Office, a dark look passed over the face of President Frank D. Gallagher.

"President Volkov, with all due respect, I don't believe a word of that. If you take me for an idiot, that's your doing. They showed up ten minutes after my men did and fired upon them. Don't toy with me, President Volkov. I know in the old world, Russia and the US didn't see eye to eye, but this is not the time for old-world politics. Get what you need to get done so I can dispatch a Globemaster to pick up my men, President Volkov. Good day," the President said, hanging up the phone.

"Sir, something wrong?" Ms. Brooks asked.

Gallagher looked at his secretary gravely. "I have a bad feeling there are bigger things at play here. Get my generals here, now."

***

Back at Aerodrom Kubinka, BlackNova 8 was sitting in a waiting room when the doctor came out.

"Sergeant Major Black is all sewn up. He had minimal damage to the peritoneum's first layer; the bullet grazed it, but it was a through and through. A couple days of rest and some antibiotics and he will be good to fly," the Russian doctor stated.

"Thank you, Doctor," Delmore said, shaking his hand.

"Well, that is good news," Smith said, looking at everyone standing in a circle.

"He said '*days*,' though—I didn't know we were staying here," Malroy added.

"We will make contact with the President and fill him in. Sergeant Delmore, do you want to take care of that?" Smith asked.

"Will do," Delmore said.

Captain Petrov walked back into the medical wing and greeted the men.

"You all will be bunking in Barracks 15. I will have Sergeant Sokolov show you where they are," Captain Petrov said as Sergeant Sokolov walked into the medical wing and nodded to all the men.

"Follow me, please," Sergeant Sokolov instructed.

All the men began to follow Sokolov to the barracks.

"Will we get some fresh clothes?" Master Corporal Kilghannon asked.

"In your barracks," Sergeant Sokolov answered bluntly.

"Russians really are cold people, eh," Corporal Malroy whispered to Master Corporal Santos.

Once they reached their barracks, Sergeant Sokolov guided them in.

"Dinner will be at the mess hall located just down and to left. Dinner is at 17:00," said Sokolov. "Any questions?"

"Yes. I need to debrief the President on the mission, and I require a phone," Delmore asked.

"Phones are for Russian military use and for President Volkov only. He has debriefed the President," Sokolov answered.

"So how will we know when we are leaving?" Delmore asked, now getting a little agitated.

"We will inform you once plans are in place," Sokolov answered as he nodded and shut the barracks door.

"Anyone else feel like we are in prison for saving the world?" Malroy said.

The barracks was a bland place—bare concrete and plain. Twelve small and cold cots lined the two walls with the feet of the cots forming a small lane down the middle. The cots were covered with gray sheets and a thin gray cotton blanket. A bathroom was located in the back right corner, but there was no shower. All the men took off their gear and changed into the plain T-shirts they were supplied with. All of them lay on their cots trying to manoeuver through Russian magazines until a knock came at the door.

"Dinnertime, gentlemen," Captain Petrov said through the door.

All the men got to their feet and proceeded to the mess hall like a line of prisoners.

"Is someone taking care of Sergeant Major Black?" Smith asked Petrov.

"Yes, he is under constant supervision," Petrov insisted.

All the men grabbed what looked like jail food—it was bland and mushy—and walked over to the far table near the back of the hall. Russian soldiers stared at them while they ate. It didn't feel like they were in prison; it was the feeling of being a zoo animal with all the base personnel's eyes on them.

"The sooner we leave, the better," Kilghannon whispered.

All the men agreed and ate their food in silence.

***

The next morning came slowly. All the men were getting dressed when another familiar face walked into their barracks.

"Good morning, men," Dr. Popov greeted.

"I have been working all day and night, but I have finally made it—the *cure*, gentlemen!" Dr. Popov said with a leap of joy. "We have worked long and hard, but we did it. We have enough for you to take back to the USA where you can continue to manufacture it. If you don't mind, join me in the briefing room so I may go over how this vaccine works."

All the men could not believe it; they had done it. Their mission was over. They all walked into the briefing room and sat down. President Volkov and Captain Petrov sat next to one another, listening intently.

"Good morning, everyone, I am going to speak English because we have company. We have done it!" said Popov. "This is the cure that will inoculate everyone who is not infected. Finally, we can stop the spread of this retched infection. We don't have a cure that reverses this infection, sadly—not yet, anyway—but at least now no one new will get infected,"

"We have it in liquid form now, but we are trying to put it into pill form for rapid distribution. Simply swallow the pill, and within fifteen hours, the subject will be protected from the airborne and bite transmutations of the infection. One thing to consider is that the berserker's strain is stronger, as we all know. Berserkers are mad, and they mutilate themselves. We have not broken that strain of the virus yet, but we are working to resolve it," Dr. Popov said, looking upon the crowd.

"When can we start inoculating people?" President Volkov asked.

"Once we put it into manufacturing. For now, we can make the liquid form and begin inoculating our troops, generals, and of course *you*, Mr. President," Popov said. "So, in finishing, we do not have a 100-percent cure for everything, but we have broken the surface, gentleman. We can finally stop the spread; now we just need to learn how to reverse it," Popov said happily.

Everyone began to clap and cheer with happiness; some began to hug Dr. Popov.

***

Later, after the meeting, Captain Petrov came to the barracks.

"We have you all leaving on a flight once your Globemaster arrives. Be ready to leave within the next four to five hours. We are prepping Sergeant Major Black for transportation, as well," Captain Petrov said.

"Also, we are leaving with some of the cure, correct?" Corporal Ryan Witter added.

'Yes, you will get your samples, as well," Captain Petrov said, shutting the door.

***

Hours later, there was another knock at the door.

"Please gather your things, your ride will be landing in twenty minutes," the voice said.

All the men gathered their gear and proceeded to the landing strip. Smith and Malroy proceeded to the medical wing to gather Sergeant Major Black.

"Gentleman," Black said in a soft, pain-filled voice.

"Johnny, how are you, brother?" Smith said, grabbing Black's gear for him.

"A lot better, still some pain, but time will heal it," Black said, slowly walking down the hall with Malroy and Smith.

Once outside, they saw the Globemaster on the runway, getting refueled.

"Home time," Malroy said with a happy tone to his voice.

President Volkov and Captain Petrov stood near the Globemaster, admiring the machine.

"Thank you, sir, for your hospitality and assistance in the mission," Black said, extending his hand to President Volkov.

"The pleasure is mine, Sergeant Major Black. Thank you for your efforts. The world is on track to being a better place," President Volkov said, smiling a crooked smile.

Sergeant Major Black then extended and shook Captain Petrov's hand and thanked him.

Once all were on board, the men happily sat back and relaxed in their chairs as the Globemaster III took off from Aerodrom Kubinka, bound for JB Anacostia-Bolling. A new sense of hope filled each and every man on that flight home. Thoughts about their families and a new life beyond this infected world didn't seem as bleak now that they could stop the spread and finally get ahead of the infection.

Sergeant Delmore held the pressurized aluminum case that contained three vials of the cure for the purpose of duplication and distribution to the public. The medical staff on the flight monitored Sergeant Major Black as he rested in the back, his health slowly getting back to normal as he recovered from the bullet wound.

9. BURNING QUESTIONS

The Globemaster landed around 02:00. Four black Suburban SUVs came onto the runway to greet the Globemaster and its passengers. Two medical agents exited the vehicle along with four secret service agents and stood in wait as the rear loading ramp began to fall. Everyone began to exit. Delmore carried the aluminum case containing the cure off the Globemaster and walked toward the medical team. Sergeant Major Black and the two medical personnel slowly walked down the ramp and were greeted by a wheelchair.

"I am not getting in that," Black said sternly.

The one medical attendant waved the lady and wheelchair away quickly. Santos and Malroy walked down the ramp and looked around.

"Good to be back in North America," Malroy chuckled.

"Yes, but not home yet," Santos added as he began to walk again, also carrying Sergeant Major Black's gear in his hand.

Once the news broke of the cure, the base atmosphere was now hopeful instead of despairing. The soldiers walked around laughing and with smiles for once instead of cold-hearted stare downs and broken half-smiles filled with fatigue.

BlackNova 8 all loaded up into the black Suburban's and headed toward the White House—all except for Sergeant Major Black, who stayed and was put into the medical wing for more observation. The medical officers took the case and began toward the fourth black Suburban, their destination being USAMRIID to further develop the cure.

On the way to the White House, Corporal Rex Witter spoke up. "Russia does have nicer drives, I must admit."

Santos and Kilghannon chuckled at the comment as they continued to look out the window at broken-down buildings, abandoned lots, and trashed street.

The convoy pulled up to the White House's front entrance and opened the doors; once again, the President's assistant Muller was there to greet them at the top of the stairs.

"Gentlemen, please follow me," Muller instructed.

Through the main lobby and down the corridor, the men walked two by two led by Delmore. They filed into the Cabinet Room where, once again, President Gallagher sat awaiting their arrival. The President stood up and clapped.

"Welcome back, gentlemen," he said.

All the men nodded as they took their at-ease stance, now standing all in a line facing the President.

"Please, you all deserve a seat for once," the President offered.

"I don't speak for all, but I have been sitting for eight hours, sir. I prefer to stand at the moment," Sergeant Delmore said sternly.

"Understandable," Gallagher said, looking at all the men.

"First and foremost, my absolute thanks to each and every one of you. Your bravery and ability to execute have saved this world from complete chaos caused by the infected. We now have the cure being mass-produced, and we will be handing it out to the public as soon as possible. Because of you men, we have a chance at survival," the President said.

"I know we are in a time in which our victory should be enjoyed, and it *will* be, but we still have some matters to table before any mass celebrations are to proceed. We have the issue of the whereabouts of doctors Clase and Sue. And I will be honest—I haven't had any luck in contacting China to give them the good news. Although I know they may not want to talk to me at the moment, considering we killed some of their men during the cure extraction mission in Russia."

"Sir, we had no intel or warning that they would be there," said Sergeant Smith. "Also, they became hostile when they fired upon us first."

"I know, Sergeant Smith, but politics are politics, and we now have Chinese blood on our hands that I will have to wash off somehow," Gallagher said. "But that is for *me* to figure out. Now," he continued, "concerning Dr. Clase and Dr. Sue, we have found all our suspicions to be correct. We have kept a close eye on Dr. Sue. He had connections with the Chinese government and was feeding them intelligence about our research and findings. Regarding Dr. Clase, I am sad and embarrassed to inform all of you that he was an informant for the Chinese government. We have reasons to suspect that he infected Jack Morrow and then staged everything."

"But he was attacked by Morrow," Delmore said.

"Yes, but Dr. Clase knew and planned this far ahead. We found notes, details, and maps on what he was doing," the President said.

All the men looked confused and amazed that this could happen.

"So, what do we do now, sir?" Ryan Witter asked.

"Now that China has our plans and intelligence about our research, I think we will be okay from now on," the President said.

All the men groaned and moaned.

"What do you mean, 'okay?'" Smith said, slamming his fist.

President Gallagher smiled and slid a file onto the table. "We gave Dr. Sue bad intelligence as soon as we were onto him and his motives for wanting to learn more about our research."

"What about Dr. Clase?" Kilghannon asked.

Delmore stood up and nodded to the President. "We were supposed to get rid of him because we were catching on to Dr. Clase as well, but the mission went south when the horde came, and we didn't get a chance."

Sergeant Smith stood up and yelled. "No more secrets, no more bullshit! Only the truth will be spoken, because in this day and age, we need the truth to overcome this epidemic. We need all the help we can get. If you suspect any more informants, we will take them in and question them," Smith said, looking at everyone.

All the men nodded and agreed and looked at the President.

Gallagher nodded. "I understand your frustration, gentlemen. But we do these things to ensure the safety of *everyone*."

"So, do we have any missions to discuss? Do we know the whereabouts of Dr. Clase or Dr. Sue?" Smith asked.

"We have our borders locked down with their faces everywhere, so if they turn up, we will apprehend them," the President said.

"Why would Dr. Clase want to do this?" Malroy asked.

"Dr. Clase was very driven, but we had a disagreement about human testing early on when this first started. I told him only lab animals for now, until we get more concrete results. He didn't like that, but he did it anyway. But once he got to human testing, we started noticing that his cures were actually transforming the human specimens. His specimens would be infected and turned into berserkers, but these berserkers were still infected, so now their bites could infect, but they had the strength of a berserker. He evolved the epidemic, so we burned all his results and made him start over."

"So, you let him start over when you knew he was messing around and not actually finding a solution, but in fact worsening the problem?" Malroy said stiffly as he slammed his fist onto the table.

"He is a brilliant man; we needed a solution, and his mind could come up with one. We played it out, and this was the best option. But from then on, we monitored his work," the President said.

"Terrific," said Santos. "Now look where we are: a mad scientist who hates you is on the loose with another scientist we don't know the status of, with military secrets he could share with the enemy."

"Like he would make it to China," Corporal Ryan Witter said.

"But if he did, or if he somehow got our secrets to them—then what? We need a nationwide search for this man," Smith said.

"There seems to be a lot of finger-pointing," Delmore said, standing up.

"We were called in to help the situation, and all you guys have done is made it worse!" Malroy said, screaming over top of everyone.

"Made it worse? We have been fighting day in and day out, trying to preserve what we have. Yes, we have made decisions that don't look so good, but don't you dare come here and point the fingers, asshole!" Delmore said, now in Malroy's face.

Malroy and Delmore eyed each other down. No one was blinking or talking.

"Everyone stand down, this is a time for cool heads!" the President demanded.

"We need a solution before this gets any worse," Smith said softly.

"Well, since we are so bad at making decisions, why don't you guys come up with the plan, and we will be your cheerleaders," Delmore said as he walked out of the room.

Kilghannon and the Witters stood in the room, looking around in discomfort.

"No more finger-pointing, alright? Let's just make a plan and see it through," Smith said, looking at all the men.

Everyone was still silent. Even the President did not know what to say.

"Listen, we need to unite together here! No more Nova and Black Fox Company, we are BlackNova 8. We need to start being one unit, just like we are in battle," Smith said sternly. Then he added, "Gentlemen, there is too much chaos in the world today for us to be fighting each other right now. We need to make peace and push forward."

Kilghannon looked at Smith with a blank face. "I think we all need to take a couple minutes and calm down; we are all strung out, lad," he said as he walked out of the room.

"Everyone, go back to JB Anacostia-Bolling and cool off. We will talk shortly after I get somewhere with China," the President said.

The Witters left the room. Malroy just threw his hands up in the air.

"Whatever, man," Malroy said as he walked out.

Santos and Smith looked at each other and shrugged.

"What now, Master Corporal Santos?" Smith asked as he bowed his head.

"Give them time, we all need a bit of time to recoup," Santos said as he walked out.

Smith sat down at the table, rubbed his face with both hands, and began looking over all the notes confiscated from Dr. Clase's lab.

"I am going to call the Prime Minister and have a chat with him," the President said, leaving Sergeant Smith alone in the room.

Sergeant Smith sat back in his chair, eyes closed, listening to the President's fading footsteps.

What am I to do? he thought.

***

The President went into his office and shut the door.

"Ashley, please get President Volkov on the line," the President asked.

Moments later, the President's phone rang.

"President Volkov, good evening," the President gestured.

"Mr. President, I trust the mission was a success in your eyes," Volkov said.

"Yes, it was, we are developing the cure we retrieved from your lab, but we have a separate issue I wish to discuss," the President said.

"Go on," Volkov said.

"I just want to make sure we are on the same page, President Volkov. Helping China would only help them exterminate what's left of the human race," Gallagher said.

"Do you want to know *why* the nukes have not gone off yet, Mr. President? It's not because your dream team of soldiers stopped anything; it is because I called President Sung and told him about the cure at my lab. I gave him hope so he would not nuke anyone at this time. I am sorry I could not tell you, Mr. President."

"You told the Chinese so we would end up fighting?" the President inquired.

"*Het.* I told President Sung so he would think I am his ally, and to show that nuking is not the way to fix this issue," Volkov explained.

"And why didn't you tell me you did this?" the President asked.

"Because I didn't want to risk any precautions you would have taken, which would have made it seem like we set up the Chinese," President Volkov explained.

"Whose side are you on, President Volkov?" Gallagher asked sternly.

"You question my intentions? I had my helicopter pick up your men and extract them—I gave them safe passage through my land! I didn't assist China in any way on their mission. Question my intentions again, Mr. President, and the next conversation we will have is one of war."

And with that, President Volkov hung up.

The President clenched his jaw as he slammed the phone down on his desk.

Ms. Brooks came rushing into the office and saw the disgruntled President. "Sir, is there anything I can do?"

The President paused as he slowly sat back in his chair. "I have China on the verge of nuking half the world, a frayed relationship with Russia, and my own country to worry about. I have the leader of my team in the medical wing, the team's morale is down, and I have no clue where Dr. Clase and Sue are. I have many questions, but no answers for anyone."

"I may have some good news, sir," Ms. Brooks said, handing over a file.

He shot his secretary a questioning look.

"The girl you wanted us to find—we found her," she said.

The President sat upright and quickly scanned the file. "Tell no one. Continue to monitor her," the President said, closing the file titled "violet."

A man ran into the room. "Sir, the border of Arlington, Virginia, is under attack and being overrun!"

"Get a hold of yourself, soldier!" the President said, putting his hand on the soldier's shoulder as he caught his breath. "Get BlackNova 8 down there now!"

***

Just as BlackNova 8 showed back up to JB Anacostia-Bolling, all the men ran to the locker room and started to get geared up. A pilot ran out to the helicopter pad and fueled the Black Hawk. Corporal Rex Witter pulled Corporal Ryan Witter's vest over him and slid his sword in. Master Corporal Santos and Corporal Malroy holstered their pistols and buttoned them in while Sergeant Smith put magazine cartridges into his ammo pouches.

All the men continued to put their gear on. One by one, they finished and headed for the helicopter pad. All the men gathered by the helicopter pad and got into the helicopter, which was waiting to liftoff.

"Ready for liftoff," the pilot said as he gave the thumbs up. Sergeant Smith returned the gesture. The helicopter lifted off and headed for the West Virginia border.

10. THE LINE

The helicopter flew over the battlefield once and turned to find a spot for a landing. Infected had charged the fence and concrete barriers so that the fence was half ripped down, and then the infected had flooded in. Gunfire could be heard from above, along with the gruesome screams of men being torn apart. Soldiers were shooting their own men after they were bitten. Soldiers were moving to hand-to-hand combat after their ammo ran out. The rain started to pour as BlackNova 8 arrived. The helicopter landed, dropped off BlackNova 8, and was quickly back in the air to avoid danger.

"Alright, spread out, we need to form a line and press these infected bastards back away from the border!" Delmore ordered.

Malroy quickly shot two infected in the skull and grabbed two soldiers to stand near him in a line.

"Hold this line and press forward!" Malroy said as he continued to shoot.

Kilghannon crouched as he walked forward, shooting infected after infected, gathering men and forming the line. Over time, the line started to get longer and longer. The Witters stood together, shooting forward and picking off infected that were ripping down fences. The base was soon cleared as the men all moved forward in a line and Delmore shot the last infected that got into the compound.

"We hold this line—nothing gets through. Our women, children, and families are behind us, we fight for them. We fight for existence, and we fight for each other!" Delmore roared as he passed his gun to a soldier who had run out of ammo and pulled out his sword.

All of BlackNova 8 handed their guns to soldiers who were weaponless and pulled out their swords.

The infected roared and groaned at the food that was in front of them. Blood dripped from their lips, infected wounds and cuts covered their bodies, their clothes were torn, and they had limbs missing, jaws unhinged, and eyes red as blood. The soldiers stared back, their spines chilled by the gaze of the infected. All the soldiers stood tall, staring death in the face. The soldiers were armed with large metal pipe pieces, large pieces of wood, and some with guns loaded with minimal ammo. Other soldiers only had their bare hands, but they had courage in their hearts. One soldier near Kilghannon was shaking so much that Kilghannon took notice and looked at him—the soldier had soiled himself.

"Stay with me, you won't get hurt," Kilghannon said.

The year was 2024, but the scene that had transpired was that of a medieval battle: two armies face to face as one charged.

Delmore raised his sword. "Kill them all!" he shouted as he ran toward the horde of infected.

All the soldiers chanted and roared as they followed their fellow brother-in-arms into the horde from hell. Delmore swung his sword back and cut into the first infected, then continued swinging, stabbing, and chopping. The soldiers with guns stayed back a little and killed the infected by shooting them in the head.

Kilghannon swung his sword back and burst forward with a fit of rage in his swing as he lopped off an infected's head. Malroy smoothly stabbed an infected through the bottom of his jaw and into its head, and then crouched down and sliced an infected's legs off. Ryan Witter sliced an infected, cutting its head in half, and looked back at Rex Witter, who waved him over. Ryan Witter ran to his brother.

He rolled over Rex's back and kicked an infected in the face and then sliced the next one beside it. Ryan ducked as his brother's sword sliced above his head and through two infected's' necks. The bloody battle raged on and on, blood squirting everywhere, covering the ground and the clothes of the soldiers.

Santos punched one infected, and then turned and sliced another infected's head off. Then he bicycle-kicked the head of an infected that was charging him. The head hit another infected in the face, causing it to stop for a moment and giving Santos that second to swing his sword around and slice it's head off.

Smith snapped one infected's neck and then stabbed another in the eye. He let out a loud cry as he went bloodthirsty, slicing infected after infected and thinking about his failure to protect Sergeant Major Black. The rage in his swings were savage, and his eyes were filled with anger. An infected lunged at him, but in the nick of time, Smith dodged it as it hit the ground. Smith held his sword up and slashed off the infected's head.

Malroy looked over his shoulder and saw a soldier getting his neck ripped out as he screamed. He ran over and slashed the infected across the face, then looked at the soldier.

"Do it," the soldier said, choking on his own blood.

Malroy paused for a moment. It seemed like everything went into slow motion as he zoned out and gazed upon the battlefield, with soldiers dying, limbs being ripped off, necks being torn apart, blood staining his boots. He slowly pulled out his pistol and looked at the soldier, who gurgled up some of his own blood. He raised his gun, and then an infected tackled him down.

Malroy dropped his weapon instantly, grabbing hold of the throat of the infected on top of him. The soldier crawled and reached for the pistol and pointed it at the infected as the infected got closer to Malroy's throat. The soldier shot the infected in the head. Then

Malroy closed his eyes, tossed the infected off him, and picked up his sword. The soldier looked at Malroy, his body starting to twitch and his eyes turning a reddish color as he turned the pistol in his shaky hand and shot himself in the head. Rain ran down Malroy's face as he stared at the soldier who had saved his life and then taken his own life so he wouldn't hurt anyone. Malroy quickly wiped his face before the blood-mixed rain could drip down into his eyes or mouth.

One infected remained, and all the men regrouped and looked at it. Malroy looked at Delmore, who looked at Santos; Santos looked at Kilghannon, who looked at Ryan Witter, who looked at his brother, who was looking at Smith. All the men nodded, and all seven men stabbed the infected at the same time.

All the soldiers started cheering and chanting, "BlackNova, BlackNova, BlackNova." The men stood in a line, looking back at the group of soldiers cheering, blood dripping from their swords as they hung down toward the ground.

A helicopter's engine was heard in the distance, and it got louder and louder as it flew closer.

"Well, that's our ride," Kilghannon said as he slid his blood-soaked blade back into its sheath.

The helicopter landed, and fresh ammo and food started to get unloaded. BlackNova 8 boarded the helicopter and started their journey home to Washington. Everyone was quiet during the ride home, wiping blood from their faces. Santos looked over at Malroy.

"Are you okay?" Santos asked.

"A soldier got bitten, then told me to shoot him, but before I could, an infected tackled me down. I held him away from me for just enough time for that soldier to shoot it in the head, then the soldier shot himself," Malroy said, staring at the ground in disbelief.

"He died a hero, Corporal Malroy. He saved one of his own so you could fight another day. Remember that," Santos said, smacking Malroy's back.

"How can you be so calm and collected? Does this shit not phase you?" Malroy burst out, staring at Santos.

"Time and place, Corporal Malroy," Santos said softly

"How? When? What time is good enough for this, when is it okay to let loose? Do you enjoy this shit or something?" Corporal Malroy said, now looking out of the helicopter window.

Santos sat quietly, as did everyone else the whole ride home.

The helicopter landed on the roof of the White House. Santos opened the sliding door and saw two men standing on the roof by the doors. All the men got out and saw Sergeant Major Black standing with a nurse beside him who was helping him.

"Sergeant Major Black!" Santos cheered as he ran over to greet his buddy. Everyone else followed as they all crowded around the major.

"How are you feeling? Are you in pain? When are you going to fight again?" Everyone swarmed Sergeant Major Black with questions.

Black chuckled and then held his stomach.

"The doctor said about two weeks. I need to do therapy and just heal inside. The bullet did some damage, but I'll be back with you guys soon," Black said, holding his wound. "How was the mission? I heard a border was overrun."

"It was in rough shape, but we got it," Ryan Witter said as they all started to walk inside.

Smith walked up to Black, staring into his eyes.

"I'm so sorry, brother," Smith pleaded, holding back his emotions. Sergeant Major Black held his hand up.

"Don't even! It wasn't your fault, Sergeant Smith, and you know it. You saved my life by grabbing me and not letting me fall to my death," Black said, slowly opening his arms. Smith chuckled and hugged Black softly.

"You are one crazy bastard," Smith whispered.

11. THE PLAN

President Gallagher walked down to the lab to talk with the Canadian scientist they had flown in to work on the cure they had obtained in Russia.

"So, how is it going, Dr. Green?" President Gallagher asked.

Dr. Richard Green was a tall, lean man with square glasses covering his blue eyes. The dark-framed glasses complemented his shaggy brown hair and dark sideburns that extended to his jawline. His facial structure was deep like a vampire's—so defined and with sunken cheekbones. He was a rather tanned white man, with his white lab coat complementing his pigment.

"I think we may have a breakthrough, sir. I have made copies of the inoculation cure to test it, and all the animals are responding very well. But I made some changes to see if we could change the classification from inoculation to a full-blown cure that reverses instead of just prohibits," Dr. Green answered.

"We can get you some human specimens, if you'd like," the President offered.

"That would help a lot, sir."

"Not that I am familiar with all of this science," Gallagher said, "but what have you changed about the inoculation cure that could make it an absolute cure?"

"Well, sir, in very simple terms, the inoculation cure stops the spread and makes you immune, like a brick wall to the infected. But I've done some tests, and if my results hold true, this new cure could actually attack the infected cells in humans, just like chemo attacks cancer cells," Dr. Green said.

"So, it's chemo for the infected?" the President said with a chuckle.

"Precisely, sir," Dr. Green said. "I have more tests to run, but I am hopeful."

"I will have some soldiers go out and get you more subjects," the President said as he left the laboratory and went back up to the main floor.

Dr. Green sat down behind his lab desk and looked at the progress Dr. Clase had made before his abrupt exit. Looking through Dr. Clase's files, Dr. Green found what looked to be a plan to disburse a new strain of the virus. Dr. Green was now whipping through pages, skimming the text. The pictures on the pages looked like battle plans—a map of the surrounding area.

Dr. Green looked impressed.

What were you doing, Dr. Clase? Dr. Green questioned as he read on.

***

Meanwhile, back at JB Anacostia-Bolling, Sergeant Major Black stood in the gym facing a punching bag. Black stared at the bag and envisioned the Chinese soldier who had shot him.

"Don't even think about it," the head doctor said as he entered the gym. Black unclenched his fist.

"Think about what, Doc? I was just looking at the punching bag," Black said innocently.

"You have another couple of days of doing nothing except healing before I sign those release forms," the doctor said, looking at Black's stomach.

Black looked at the doctor. "Do you think I will fight again like I used to?"

The doctor smiled. "They fixed a lot of the tissue damage and got all the fragments of the bullet out, so it's just a matter of time, Sergeant Major Black. Just take it easy." The doctor patted Black's shoulder.

"Thank you, Doctor," Sergeant Major Black said.

"They thought they lost you when they first heard you had been shot, so be thankful you are here. You got someone looking down on you," the doctor said, smiling as he started to walk away.

Grateful, Black laughed silently to himself. *Yes, I do*, he thought as he clutched the silver cross that was around his neck.

***

Later that day, all the men's pagers went off. Almost instantly, all the men were gathered in the mission room at JB Anacostia-Bolling.

"Alright, men, it was first brought to my attention months ago, but I waited to tell you until it had been confirmed." The President paused and cleared his throat before continuing over the giant screen in the mission room. "China has lost approximately twenty of their mobile nuclear weapons to a rogue general by the name of Jiang Maiyong, and we have evidence that they are planning to get rid of the infected people, and . . ." the President paused once more, bowing his head.

He continued, "We don't have much intel on Maiyong, and what we do have is about four years out of date; however, according to our intelligence, China has been trying to negotiate with General Maiyong and his forces, giving them food and water, free passage and shelter, but they feel that they want to bomb the surrounding countries with their short-ranged nukes. From what we have found, the surrounding countries are, in fact, a highly infected population, but nevertheless, if nuclear war breaks out, this outbreak won't be the end of the human race," the President said in a heartbroken tone.

All the men sat in their chairs, stunned. The room filled with silence as all the men looked around staring at each other.

"So, what is this, then? We have to help China get their nukes back because *they* can't, and then maybe they use them against us later?" Kilghannon said.

The President lifted his head and looked at Kilghannon. "I know you men were just there, but we need to stop Maiyong and his forces before they create bigger world issues that we can't come back from. If they fire from China onto the surrounding border countries, China will be targeted by half of Asia. Russia is already tense about the situation and has been doing recon on their end, sharing information with us day to day," President Gallagher said.

"Would Russia assist again?" Malroy asked.

"Yes, President Volkov will assist in the logistics and getting us in and out."

"How come General Maiyong hasn't already set them off?" Black asked.

"We think it is because they are getting water, food, and shelter from the Chinese government, but their resources are wearing thin, and once they have nothing to offer, the short-ranged nukes go off," the President said.

Black slowly got to his feet and looked at each man in the room.

"Does this General Maiyong have a base? A compound? How many troops are at his disposal?" Black asked.

"He has a compound; Russia thinks they have fifty to eighty armed men," the President said.

"And China can't go in guns blazing because Maiyong would just detonate them," Black said.

"Correct, Sergeant Major Black," the President said.

"Even if we go in stealthily, sir, how many mobile units does this guy have? We can't hit all them at once," Black said.

"China has told Russia they can shut down the GPS systems in the missiles for ten minutes, rendering them useless, but they said only ten minutes. No less, and no more," the President said.

"Ten minutes to find the General Maiyong and kill him before he blows up half of Asia," Malroy said. "Simple enough."

The President looked around the room.

"We have a duty to protect these people, and to give them hope, no matter how little it may be, gentlemen. We may not be on talking terms with China at the moment, but this isn't just about the USA and Canada anymore. Millions of lives are at stake here," the President said.

"Now, wait a minute," Delmore said. "We need to talk this out."

"There are nukes itching to go off, and we are the most qualified to actually have a chance," Santos said.

"We need more than just us eight, for god's sake! We are talking about a nuclear-armed compound in China, and you don't think it's heavily guarded by whatever resources they have?" Delmore exclaimed.

"When would we be executing this mission, sir?" Rex Witter asked.

"I want you all on a plane tomorrow to Russia, and on the plane, you can go over mission details," the President replied.

"Gentlemen, look outside. Look at what we have done. You guys have fought so hard to return all our lives to normal. Every soldier is breaking his or her back for the return of hope. If news gets out that there is some insane general looking to blow up Asia, we will have lost everything." The President was now choking up and fighting back tears. "I know I am asking a lot. I'm asking for you all to suit up and go fight against the odds, but you are fighting these odds for the only reason I would ask you to—and that's for the sake of the human race."

Everyone started looking at each other with a sense of hope.

"If we don't do this, everything we have done means nothing," Rex Witter said under his breath.

"All the men we have lost, the friends who lost their lives to this hell, every woman, child, and man who died trying to protect one another . . . It means nothing if those nukes go off!" Kilghannon said, slamming his fist on the table.

"Let's do this!" he said, standing tall and proud.

Rex and Ryan followed Master Corporal Kilghannon's lead.

"Let's!" Santos said, smiling as he rose from his chair.

Malroy stood, looking around the room. "I've got nothing but you guys. Where you go, I go."

Sergeant Smith knew this mission could be the one he didn't come home from. He knew the night they leave could be his last night. He slowly got up from his chair as Delmore did, almost as if he and Delmore were having the same thoughts and coming to the same conclusion, which only made Smith feel like he was doing the right thing. Sergeants Smith and Delmore nodded to everyone.

"Let's get planning, then," Sergeant Major Black said. "Make this bulletproof and simple, in and out."

12. HEARTBROKEN

The sky turned dark as night fell, and all the men were in their bunks to digest and mentally prepare themselves for the mission to come.

The mission was the most dangerous yet; casualties were going to play a part in this mission. They were going to China to stop an insane rogue general from unleashing a nuclear apocalypse.

The President placed a call to China and finally had an amicable conversation with President Sung.

"President Sung, thank you for taking my call!" President Gallagher said.

"Mr. President," Sung said softly.

"I want to first apologize for the friendly fire that happened in Russia," Gallagher offered.

"Thank you, I understand there was confusion with both parties," Sung replied.

"Yes, President Sung, I gave no order to fire upon Chinese soldiers in any situation, I assure you."

"How can I help you, Mr. President?" Sung asked.

"I have been in talks with Russia, and we are planning an attack on General Maiyong on your behalf. I apologize for this, but there is no time for politics. I understand we need to talk about the events

111

that have transpired, but for now, I need military access for my men to go in and stop Maiyong."

"You kill my men, and now you demand military access across my land," President Sung replied.

"President Sung, we can have this conversation later, but Jiang Maiyong is holding your government hostage, and we need to act fast. I want a good relationship to come from this President Sung, but right now I need to do what's right for the world, not to fix what happened in Russia. We are coming to China, and we are going to stop this rogue general. You can either assist, or watch out," the President demanded.

Phone silence filled the line for what seemed like minutes.

"You have China's support, but do not forget, Mr. President, if you do not disrespect me, we will have words when this situation is under control," President Sung said as he hung up.

***

BlackNova 8 was the last hope to save the human race. Four sons of America: Master Corporal Kilghannon, Corporals Rex and Ryan Witter, and Sergeant Delmore. Four sons of Canada: Sergeant Smith, Sergeant Major Black, Master Corporal Santos, and Corporal Malroy. These eight men were about to engage in the most hectic, violent, and rage-filled fight since the epidemic began, and they all knew that if they wanted to survive, they would have to call upon every survival instinct in their bodies to make it through the hell that had come upon them.

The day broke through the morning clouds. All the men were up at the first ray of sunlight and sat in the mission room with their mission advisor, a colonel by the name of Ryder.

"Good morning, men. I have made a battle plan, and I feel it will be a good strike that is fast and will catch them off-guard," Ryder said. "After a lot of communication between China and Russia, we have a tri-nation battle plan. The objective is to kill the General Maiyong and secure all mobile missile sites. You men will be flying back to Russia, but instead of Moscow Oblast, you will be landing in a small area named 'Borzya.' This is about 164 miles from Maiyong's compound located in Hailar, China. Once you land in Borzya, Russia will take over. Captain Petrov will lead his Russian team to the first mobile site that has about seven or eight mobile missile launch vehicles. The compound you men are hitting—with the support of twenty marines—is guarded by most of General Maiyong's men, approximately thirty-five to fifty hostiles. Remember, there are civilians in the compound, so be mindful, gentleman, and pick your targets carefully. With China's intelligence unit, or what's left of it, The Chinese intelligence unit will black out the GPS locators on the missiles, but remember that they can only lock them out for a maximum of ten minutes. Once they lock the missiles, The Targets will be alerted something is happened.

"Act fast, neutralize Maiyong and his forces, and secure all mobile launchers. China has a team hitting a second off-sight location. You will be parachuting one klick from the compound. Once you call for evacuation," Ryder said, "we will have three Kamov Ka-29s on standby. They will be your ticket out once the mission is complete.

"So, in summary, gentlemen, fly to Borzya. The flight to Hailar compound will be just under an hour. Parachute down, one klick from compound. Once you reach the compound, Sergeant Major Black will give us the signal, and China will lock everything down. Orders are to kill the general and secure the missiles. Once the mission is complete, you will call for an evacuation and be taken back to the forward operations base in Borzya." Colonel Ryder looked around the room. "Questions?"

"Are we to do anything with the other teams, sir?" Corporal Ryan Witter asked.

"No—it's a three-team operation, but separate objectives," said the colonel. "The Russian team is securing one site, and the Chinese team is securing the other while we kill Maiyong and secure the four missiles they have in the compound."

All the men nodded; they understood what needed to be done.

"You will all have translators given to you, so you will be able to read the Chinese writing," Ryder said. "As for who strikes where, your entry plans, and your teams, I felt those decisions should be left to your leader, Sergeant Major Black—he knows you men best, and as a team, you all know who should do what."

"Understood," Sergeant Major Black said and nodded.

Colonel Ryder left the room, and all the men followed.

"It is a long flight, gentlemen; I will brief on the flight. Make your calls, pack your gear. Wheels up in thirty minutes," Sergeant Major Black instructed.

The Globemaster was ready: packed, all gassed up, and the pilots sitting in the cockpit. All the men boarded the Globemaster, and the rear ramp slowly began to close.

"Goodbye, America," Corporal Ryan Witter said under his breath; the last glimpse he could possibly have of his home was the runway that the Globemaster was about to take off from.

"Seatbelts on, gentlemen. Begin takeoff," the pilot came over the PA system.

All the men strapped in and felt the rumble as the engines engaged. The Globemaster began to shake as it reached faster and faster speeds, then all the men felt the wheels leave the ground. No longer on American soil, each man felt uneasy in the pit of his stomach. The fact that some of them might not return home wasn't lost on any of them.

About an hour into the flight, all the men were chatting, telling battle stories, and sharing chuckles. It almost seemed normal, like the fate of the world wasn't weighing down on their shoulders. Malroy and Santos sat next to one another, talking about the day they had met in the CPR training course, how Santos thought Malroy was the class clown, which held true to this day. Malroy was proud to say he brought comedy to every mission. Malroy brought up a time when it was the Army vs. the Navy in an ice hockey tournament, and how Santos was a terrible skater. Santos was never taken for a chump, though; after the first game, Santos rented the ice all weekend and practiced skating. When the next game rolled around, Santos was skating circles around some of the men.

Delmore was reading in the corner with his glasses on when Kilghannon walked over.

"You really show your age when you wear those," Kilghannon laughed.

Delmore was not fazed by Kilghannon's comment. "Wisdom, my friend, wisdom with age."

Kilghannon looked around the plane—some of the men he had just met, and now they held a place in his heart; and the others, who he had known for years, continued to hold a place in his heart. Kilghannon looked over at Delmore again. "We have fought together for years. You ever think about moments when you thought that was it for you?"

Delmore removed his glasses and pondered for a moment. "Iraq, 2007, on patrol, when the front Humvee flew to the sky right in front of us. That goddamn IED—that was the first explosion I had heard that close. My ears rang, and it was just the sound—they actually hurt from the ringing noise. I remember being so disorientated that I didn't know where my weapon was, or where anyone was, for the matter. Then I remember you grabbed me from the passenger seat, bullets hitting the door as you dragged me behind the vehicle and handed me a rifle. Asking me if I could hear you, and then that *second* explosion happened. Right before it hit, you yelled 'RPG!' I thought we were done for, Eddie, I really did."

Kilghannon was silent for a moment, and then looked at Delmore. "That was a crazy day. We lost Higgins and Marsh that day. It's never easy losing someone—one moment you're laughing, and then you look over and half of their face is charred black. I never really process it until I'm alone," Kilghannon said, now looking at his feet and bent over with his elbows on his knees.

Delmore put his hand on Kilghannon's back. "I don't think we ever get over it, brother. We just go numb so we can do our job."

***

Meanwhile, back at the White House, the President gathered his generals.

"Gentleman, we have BlackNova in the sky, and the pilot has confirmed they are five hours away," the President said as they all got seated in the situation room.

"Dr. Clase and Dr. Sue are confirmed in China; we do not know how they got there, or who helped them, but it is confirmed that they are there. Does BlackNova know to locate them?" Navy General Watts asked.

"Their mission is to stop nuclear war, and anything else is secondary," the President said. "Now, how are we doing here at home, gentlemen?"

"We have confirmation from our outpost that all borders are secure. No infection threats for about three days. The city is infection-free, and walls are being built for precaution. We have survivors appearing daily, though, it is putting hardship on food and water resources," Resource Minister Kline explained.

"We need to do a push for more cities to be cleared. We need our cities back so we can start rebuilding," Gallagher explained.

"Sir, we are doing our best, but we have a lack of communication, society has completely fallen, and we are trying to restore order. Small tribes have formed on the outskirts of the cities, and we have government troops fighting citizens. It's become every man for himself out there. Also, a lack of trust is a huge issue, sir," General Cousins explained.

The President paused for a moment and looked around the room; the men's faces were tired but determined, just like his.

"Put out an announcement," President Gallagher said. "Tell our citizen's we are here to help. We are here to establish order. Send spokespeople to these tribes you speak of and ask them to go back into the city and rebuild. We must unite; if BlackNova completes this mission, the race will be on for who can recover first. We need to come out on top and be the superpower again," the President ordered.

13. THE BEGINNING OF THE END

Sergeant Smith sat next to Sergeant Major Black.

"Everyone, gather around," Sergeant Major Black ordered.

All the men gathered and began to listen.

"When we drop into hostile territory, we move single file to the compound. Intelligence has given us a map of the compound. The layout is as follows. It is a big square compound—pretty basic, actually. The front gate is on the south side, and barbed wire covers the top of the walls. Once through the front gate, on the west side, there are gardens and a pathway leading to the back of the living quarters. On the east side is a structure that we think is used as an office—an administrative building. There is a pathway that divides the compound right down the middle. When you head north, up the pathway, you will see living quarters, six huts, and we presume civilians will be occupying them. I want six marines to secure the civilians, I do not want one civilian killed. On the right side of the pathway is a mess hall and a workshop. The prize is at the back—the northwest and northeast corners are where the missiles are. Each corner has a guard tower, and I want those cleared out. The less fire coming down on us, the better," Black said.

He continued, "Once we make contact with the compound, I want two marines on each guard tower. Once cleared, take up a position there and provide cover for us on the ground. Once we take out the guards, we charge the front gate. Blow the charges and converge on the compound. Go up the center pathway and break off; corporals Witter and Witter, take three marines with you to the west side of the compound, secure the living quarters. Master corporals Santos and Kilghannon and Corporal Malroy, take two marines and go to the east side, securing the mess hall and workshop. Sergeants Delmore, Smith, and myself will continue forward toward the nukes with the remaining seven marines. When we get the end of the pathway, Sergeant Delmore will take three marines and secure the northwest nukes, and Sergeant Smith and I will take the remaining marines and secure the northeast nukes. We are all to be on the lookout for General Maiyong and to dispatch him on sight. Any questions?"

"Are there infected, sir?" a marine asked.

"This is an element we are unsure of, but be prepared to fight both compound hostiles and the infected," Black said.

"Once all objectives are completed, I will order the extraction. Extraction point is the gardens, in the southwest corner of the compound. I will alert everyone when I have called for extraction. As always, gentlemen, wounded first. Set a perimeter around the gardens and protect until all are extracted. Sergeant Delmore and I will be the last to leave to ensure no one is left behind. Watch each other's six, and let's get home together as we came," Sergeant Major Black finished.

"Yes, sir!" All the men roared.

"Thirty minutes to the landing strip in Borzya," the pilot said over the intercom.

"Gear up, boys, check each other's packs. Safety your weapons, and turn on translators. The translators will help when we land in Russia, as well," Black said.

All the men began to scurry, putting on all their gear. Black walked away from everyone and slowly pulled out a picture of his daughter and wife. Smith came up behind him.

"They will be looking over you, brother," Smith said, putting his hand on Black's shoulder.

"I know—sometimes I wish they wouldn't," Black mumbled as he tucked the picture in his breast pocket.

Sergeant Smith grabbed the satellite phone from the receiver and dialed the Comox Base.

"Comox 19, how may I direct your call?" the receptionist said.

"Laura Smith, extension 2943," Sergeant Smith answered.

The phone rang three times before a sweet, soft, angel-like voice filled Brock Smith's eardrum.

"Baby, is that you?" Laura asked.

"Yeah, baby, it's me," he said, holding back emotions. Laura always felt better knowing he was confident.

"Rose, come here, baby, Daddy's on the phone," Laura shouted.

"Daddy?" a little girl's voice came over the phone.

"Hi, baby, how's my little monster?" Smith chuckled.

"Good, me and mommy had an infection drill today, and I got to run around the base," Rose said.

"Oh, so you are well prepared now, aren't you, sweetheart?" Smith chuckled.

"Yeah! Daddy, when are you coming home?" Rose asked with her sweet little voice. "Mommy makes me cry when she cries, Daddy."

Smith was now clenching his jaw, and his heart ached. All he ever wanted was to be home again with his wife and daughter.

Struggling to hold it together, Smith managed to get out, "Soon, baby, soon I promise."

"Okay, Daddy."

"Listen, baby, Daddy has to go fight some monsters. I will call when Daddy is done, okay?" he said.

"Okay, bye, Daddy. I love you!" Rose said

"It's never goodbye, sweetheart," Smith said as he waited for Laura to return to the phone.

"You be safe, and you come home to us, you hear?" Laura said, fighting back tears.

"Always, my love, always," Smith said as his eyes began to water.

120

"I don't care what you have to do, Brock," Laura said. "You do it."

"Yes, ma'am," Smith said with a moment of silence between them. "I love you, baby, we will talk soon," he said and hung up the phone.

***

Laura heard the dial tone as she whispered, "I love you too."

She went over to her bedroom where Rose was sitting on the end of her bed and shut the door. Sliding down the door, she began to cry, her body shaking as she tried to gain control of herself. Now on her knees, Laura put her hands together.

"He has made it this far—please don't take him from me now," she whispered, grabbing her crucifix that was around her neck.

***

"Seatbelts, everyone, we are landing," the pilot said as everyone grabbed their seats and held on. The Globemaster began to shake as they began their descent.

The Globemaster made contact with the ground and bounced twice before completely grounding itself. It came to a halt, and the rear ramp began to open after a nine and a half hour flight.

"Let's go, boys!" Sergeant Major Black said as he led his men out of the plane.

Captain Petrov and Sergeant Sokolov stood with their men all geared up and ready.

"Sergeant Major Black, glad to see you walking again," Petrov said, shaking his hand.

"Thank you, I'm glad to be standing. Everything ready?" Black asked, looking around.

"Ready when you are, Major."

"Let's do it," Black said.

"Saddle up, gentlemen," Black said as he pointed to the Kamov Ka-29s.

All the marines and BlackNova 8 began to fill up the helicopters.

"Sergeant Major Black, a word," Petrov said.

"Yes?"

"Good luck. We may see differently on points, live different lives, and our countries may not be friends. But this day, we are brothers," Captain Petrov said, staring deep into Sergeant Major Black's eyes.

"Brothers," Black said as they grabbed each other's forearms and nodded before going their separate ways.

All the men looked around as the helicopters began to lift off.

"Help each other and check each other's parachutes three minutes before the jump," Sergeant Major Black roared.

The men gave a unified "Hoorah!" It was supposed to be a forty-five-minute ride, but what it felt like was ten minutes. All the men were silent, focused and mentally prepared for the battle that was heading their way. Black looked at Smith; they'd been on too many missions together to count, and those countless dances with death had given them an unspeakable bond. They locked eyes. Black nodded; Smith nodded back. Night came over the helicopter; it was a darkness that matched every soldier's heart in that helicopter.

"Three minutes to drop point!" the pilot shouted.

All the men unstrapped themselves and hooked up each other's parachutes. Sergeant Major Black stood at the start of the jump line.

"Night vision on, eyes on me!" Black shouted as the side door was tossed open.

Santos bowed his head and grabbed his cross. "Forgive me, Father, for I am about to sin. Give me the strength to kill, not in your name but in mine. I shall pay for my sins upon our meeting but for now provide me strength my lord," he said and tucked his crucifix into his shirt.

The wind was powerful as the men stood in two columns. Black and Delmore looked down, while Smith and Kilghannon stood behind them, watching the red light, waiting for it to turn green. When it did, Kilghannon and Malroy put their hands on the shoulders of Delmore and Black. That was the cue. The men all started walking and started jumping off, "I'll see you down there old man" Malroy chuckled as he turned to face Kilghannon as he began to fall off the helicopter flipping him off.

"You little piece of shit." Kilghannon laughed as he jumped off the helicopter.

Ryan and Rex Witter were next.

"We got this," Rex said as he fist-bumped Ryan.

Ryan winked at his brother as he turned his back to the open ramp and fell off with a smile on his face. Rex laughed, as he was the last to jump.

"Package drop point reached," the pilot said.

The men formed up in the shape of an arrowhead as they fell. Black watched the altitude on his watch as the release point crept closer and closer. Black then gave the signal to spread out and pulled his release string. His parachute shot up and opened quickly, jolting him up. He let out a grunt of pain as the jolt hurt his stomach wound. Gliding down and aiming for the compound, all the men, for the first time, smelled fresh air as they slowly fell toward the earth.

After ten minutes of gliding down, all the men had their boots on the ground.

Grabbing their weapons, the men formed a circle and crouched quietly for a moment to listen for any disturbance: infected groans, people talking, or any big animals. All the men scanned the trees around them, but no heat signals were noted.

"Blackbird to nest, blackbird is out of the nest," Black whispered as he continued to scan the tree line.

"Nest to blackbird, blackout to commence once secondary nest is located," a Russian man said over the radio.

Black pointed to the ground, signaling everyone to lie down.

Sergeant Major Black then signaled forward, and all the men began walking in a single line toward General Maiyong's compound.

14. DO OR DIE

"Blackbird to nest. We have secondary nest in sight. Awaiting the cue," Black whispered.

All the men lay belly down on a little grassy hill, near the south wall of the compound. The front gate looked heavily guarded. Each guard in all four of the guard towers continued to scan the surrounding area.

Black signaled two marines to the left, and two marines to the right.

"We need to take out the guard towers. Pick your targets, and wait for my command," Black said over the radio.

The marines scurried across the grassy terrain until they all had view of a guard tower and their future targets. One by one, the marines radioed their targets until all four guards were accounted for and ready to be assassinated. All the men waited, and their hearts, although not racing, were beating hard against their chests.

Captain Petrov came over the radio. "Russian Bird in position, awaiting order."

Moments passed with silence as all the men waited for the go-ahead.

"Assault!" a man came over the radio.

"Copy that," Black confirmed.

124

"Take out the guards," Black ordered.

A few seconds later, the marines confirmed their fatal shots. Black gave the signal to press forward toward the front gate.

"Marines who killed the tower guards, take up your positions in the towers," Black ordered.

All the men scurried to the wall that was the front gate, leaning their backs up against the wall. Malroy and Santos placed charges on the front gate. Santos looked at Black, who had to give the signal to blow it. Black paused for a moment, then looking at Santos, gave him the nod.

"And here we go . . . Fire in the hole!" Santos roared.

A loud bang and minor flares of fire filled the night sky as the front gate busted off its hinges and collapsed to the ground. Black entered the smoky entrance first with his C7 assault rifle in front of him. Loud screams began to ring out. Chaos had erupted in the compound.

"Team 1 Rex/Ryan, move now and secure civilians!" Black ordered.

The Witters broke off from the front gate assault with three additional marines and began toward the west side of the compound. Gunfire was exchanged.

Ryan Witter ran up against the side of the first civilian building and peered around the corner.

"Sergeant Major Black, we got a kid here shooting at us!" Witter reported while under fire.

"Dispatch all enemies," Black ordered.

Bullets began to pelt the house Ryan was leaning against. Ryan turned the corner again and was about to shoot the child when he hesitated and returned to his hidden position.

"Fuck . . . Fuck . . ." Ryan muttered to himself.

Then more roars could be heard; more men were coming to defend their compound. Rex pulled Ryan away from the edge of the house, taking his spot. Rex turned the corner and returned fire, planting a bullet in the head of the child.

For a moment, Ryan stood in shock at his brother's actions, and how easily they had come to be.

"Press forward!" Rex ordered.

Back in the front, gunfire rained on BlackNova 8 and the marines.

"Team 2, break off!" Black ordered as he returned to his standing position and returned gunfire, covering Team 2.

Santos, Malroy, and Kilghannon, along with their two additional marines, ran for the east side of the compound, toward the office building. Santos peered around a corner and quickly waved the two marines forward. Malroy followed, and as he ran, a man jumped from an open door, tackling him to the ground. Santos took aim, but couldn't get a clear shot until Malroy held the man's head up and away from himself. Santo planted a bullet in the man's skull and proceeded to help Malroy up. Kilghannon, now at the front of the squad, moved into the office building, where a brigade of bullets began raining down on them.

"Take cover!" Kilghannon roared.

Back at the front gate, Smith and Delmore exchanged fire with three Chinese who were hiding behind a truck, firing blind.

"Flank!" Smith roared as he began to run to the left of the truck.

Delmore ran to the right. Bullets flew by them as they reached the truck. The Chinese stood to defend themselves, but they were gunned down by Smith and Delmore, who then took cover behind the truck as more Chinese came out and fired upon them.

"Marines, press forward!" Black ordered.

All additional seven marines pressed forward through the firefight to gain ground.

Rex and Ryan entered the first civilian building and began to look around.

"Down! Down! Down!" Rex barked as he shoved women and children to the floor.

Women and children cried in terror as all the men entered the first building. A Chinese man ran into the building and stabbed a marine in the back repeatedly; the marine fell to his knees, screaming in pain. Ryan turned and quickly got off three rounds into the Chinese man, who collapsed instantly, dropping his blood-soaked knife.

"Man down!" Ryan shouted as he ran toward the marine.

The marine was the first casualty; blood gurgled from his mouth as he choked on it. Ryan pulled out his gun and placed it on his head.

"Sorry, brother," Ryan said as he shot the marine in the head, ending his suffering.

Two Chinese continued to shoot at Santos, Malroy, and Kilghannon from the stairs as they took cover behind an office reception desk.

"Give me some cover fire, I'll end this," Kilghannon said as he got ready to stand up.

Santos and Malroy blind fired, causing the Chinese to stop and seek cover. Kilghannon stood up and quickly shot both in their legs as they tried to make it upstairs. Both men fell in pain and began to try and crawl, but were quickly dispatched by Kilghannon. The two marines entered and began upstairs with Santos behind them. Malroy and Kilghannon searched the office for more hostiles.

Near the middle of the compound, a loud, unified cry came from the barracks as Chinese began to pour out shooting chaotically.

I knew it was too easy, Black thought.

"Hold here!" Black said as he ran and slid behind cover, adopting a crouching position and firing upon the mob.

"We got a lot of hostiles now, be alert," Black instructed.

"We need to disperse the mob!" Smith roared as he began covering from the continuous rain of bullets.

"Run to Black!" Delmore yelled to Smith.

Smith ran across an open area, dodging gunfire. Delmore unscrewed the gas cap on the truck and jumped into the driver seat. Bullets shattered the windshield as Delmore threw the Nissan Tundra into drive and floored it toward the mob.

"What is he doing?" Black asked.

Delmore closed in on the mob.

"Hit the gas tank when I'm clear!" Delmore came over the radio.

"Oh, *that's* what he's doing," Smith said recovering from his slide into cover.

Delmore then kicked open the driver door and dove out. Before the Chinese soldiers could begin to shoot Delmore, Sergeant Major Black stood and shot the open gas tank of the truck, which instantaneously erupted flames, causing an explosion. Delmore covered his head with his hands and felt the heat from the explosion on the back of his neck.

"Fuck me, it worked," Delmore laughed to himself as he regained his footing and quickly ran toward the school building for cover.

Ryan and Rex were still rounding up the civilians when Ryan paused.

"Sir, are civilians supposed to have ropes tied to their hands?" Ryan Witter said over the radio.

"Come again?" Black said, laying down more fire upon the mob.

"The civilians, they are tied up, sir. I don't think they are here by choice," Ryan said.

Black was now sidetracked, pondering to himself why they would be tied up if they were supposed to be free people here fighting the Chinese government.

"Are they *all* tied up?" Black asked, now taking cover as Smith and Delmore continued to fight.

Ryan and Rex looked around the hut.

"You two, check the other hut now!" Rex Witter ordered.

The two marines left the hut and entered the next one. Seconds passed, and then one marine came over the radio.

"Sir, they are tied up here, too," the marine stated.

"Keep them tied up for now, converge on the center of the compound and help us get rid of this mob," Black ordered.

"Yes, sir!" Ryan Witter said as he and his brother left the hut to join the gunfight.

Santos and two marines walked down the hallway of the office building, coming up to the first room. Santos nodded to a marine as he stepped back and kicked the door in. Santos entered first and quickly shot a Chinese man in the head. Falling instantly, his weapon clanked against the floor.

"Clear, next room," Santos ordered.

One marine in the northeast guard tower stopped firing to reload when he quickly took a look around; looking outside the compound toward the tree line, he noticed something moving. He paused for a moment to focus in on the moving object when his heart fell into his stomach.

"Infected incoming, I repeat infected incoming. Northeast side," the marine reported over the radio.

Black paused when he heard the news over the radio, then he shook his head. *Nothing ever comes easy.*

"Guard towers," he ordered, "refocus your fire and protect the perimeter of the compound. We need a clean escape. No infected within the compound."

"Yes, sir!" all the marines shouted as they refocused their fire toward the incoming infected.

Malroy and Kilghannon were searching the office when they came across a folder with Dr. Clase written on the top.

"Master Corporal, do you see this?" Malroy said as he handed the folder to Kilghannon.

"Why do they have *his* research?" Kilghannon asked.

Both men stood for a moment when they heard a deep groan from the basement.

"I didn't like the sound of that," Malroy said as he turned his attention to the stairs leading to the basement.

"Santos, I am heading to the basement. Malroy is on the main level still," Kilghannon stated as he raised his assault rifle and headed toward the stairs.

"Keep this floor clear," Kilghannon ordered.

"Yes, sir!" said Malroy.

"Sergeant Major Black, we found folders with Dr. Clase's name on it in the office here," Malroy said.

Black's thoughts began to rise. Why were the civilians tied up? Why was Dr. Clase's name on a folder? Were the Chinese hiding something?

The Witters and their two marines joined the firefight from the west, now flanking the mob of eight Chinese compound residents.

Smith tossed a grenade in the air, and it exploded right in the middle of the mob, perfectly tossed. Screams of pain filled the chaotic night air as the fire slowly came to a stop. Smith stood up and fired one last shot into the last Chinese resident's head.

"Push forward!" Black said as they all crouched and pressed down the pathway toward the nukes.

"Sir, more infected are converging on our position!" a marine stated.

"Rex and Ryan, front gate now! Nothing gets by!" Black ordered.

Rex and Ryan took their marines and ran to the front gate that had been blasted open. The iron doors lay hanging, barely on their hinges.

"Push the other door, brother. We will close them best we can!" Rex exclaimed as he began pushing the heavy door closed. The doors touched at the top, but did not meet at the bottom due to being badly damaged.

"They will have to filter through, take turns. Once empty, call it out and reload. If they get in, we are fucked," Ryan said as he aimed his C7 rifle at the V-shaped opening.

Santos opened the second door on the right of the hallway slowly as he entered. No one was in the room, but there were world maps with pins in key locations around Asia.

"Sergeant Major Black, I think I found their targets for the nukes," Santos stated as he studied the map. The two marines carried on to the next room to clear it.

In the basement, Kilghannon came to a metal door—not the type you usually see in an office.

"Guys, I think I got something here—" Kilghannon radioed, when suddenly a loud growl and bang smashed the door.

"Oh, yeah . . . I got something," Kilghannon stated.

Kilghannon backed up with his C7 trained on the door as the banging continued, and the metal started to deform from the force of the blows.

"Corporal Malroy, be aware. We got some type of animal in the basement," Kilghannon said as he gripped his rifle tighter.

Santos looked around the room, rifling through papers—he kept seeing Dr. Clase's name at the top of papers.

Could Clase be in the compound?

"Corporal Ryan Witter, when you were in the living quarters, what were the people yelling? Did you have your translator on?" Master Corporal Santos asked.

"Yes, sir, they were asking for help," Ryan Witter answered quickly.

"Sergeant Major Black, something isn't right here," Santos stated.

Black and his team approached the end of the pathway; the barracks were ahead.

"Marines, clear the barracks," Black ordered. "Sergeant Delmore, northwest nukes. Go."

As the marines entered the barracks, gunfire sprung up again,

"Infected!" a marine exclaimed over the radio.

Infected . . . in the barracks? Black thought.

"Guard towers, report," Black ordered.

"Infected still coming, but contained," a marine reported.

"Ryan and Rex how is the front gate?" Black asked.

"Stable, sir. No infected in the compound," Rex said.

Black thought back to the briefing notes, and how scarce and woefully out of date the information on Jiang Maiyong was.

"Team, keep an eye out for Dr. Clase," said Black. "I think he is actually the so-called rogue general, and that Maiyong is just a cover."

"Horde, southeast tower!" a marine yelled.

Corporal Ryan and Rex Witter fixed their attention on the front gate. The groans and roars could be heard as the infected sprinted toward the front gate.

"Hold this line, gentlemen. Not one gets by us!" Ryan roared, cocking his rifle.

The marines gave a war cry as the infected began pouring through the V-shaped opening in the front gate.

"Contact, front gate!" Rex roared over the front gate.

Smith and Black proceeded to the nukes in the northeast corner. Black felt a shiver go up his spine when he came to the nukes—they had *already* been disabled.

"Has anyone touched the nukes yet?" Black asked.

Everyone reported negative.

Then, out of the night skies, two helicopters could be heard coming closer to the compound.

"I need a visual on those helicopters, now!" Black demanded.

Malroy heard the call and began sprinting toward the stairs, up three floors and then burst through the roof access door.

"Corporal Malroy on the roof, sir. I cannot see the flags on the side yet," Malroy said as he continued to look.

"My nukes have been disarmed, as well," Delmore said, confirming Black's worst fear.

"It's a trap!" Black roared.

Bullets began to pelt the rooftop around Malroy, who sprinted toward cover under heavy gunfire.

"Russians!" Malroy said over the radio.

"Control, this is Blackbird. It's a trap!

Black waited but heard nothing. "Control, this is Blackbird, do you copy?"

"They have cut our radio contact," Black cried. "If they aren't in American fatigues, kill them."

Rex and Ryan, at the front gate, started to become overwhelmed.

"Marines, to the front gate! Help them!" Black ordered, now re-examining the battlefield.

All seven marines began to run down the pathway toward the front gate. Two missiles fired and destroyed the school and mess hall, rocking the compounding.

"Santos, Malroy, Kilghannon, get out of the office building now!" Black ordered.

Malroy gained his footing and saw a helicopter coming back around.

"Shit, shit, shit . . ." Malroy said as he ran toward the edge of the building with bullets landing right behind him.

Malroy jumped off the edge, not even looking down. As he fell, he thought that was it, until he hit a tent, crashing through it and smashing a desk. Malroy groaned and slowly got to his feet. He was in a world of pain, but there was no time to address it.

"Bring those helicopters down!" Black ordered as a missile flew by him and blew up the barracks behind him, blasting him forward and to the ground.

"Johnny!" Smith said as he ran toward his friend. Delmore began firing on the helicopter, causing it to turn away.

"Kilghannon, bring those bastards down!" Delmore shouted.

"Working on it, sir!" Kilghannon reported.

"Master Corporal Santos, tell me when the helicopter is near the west side of the office building. I'm bringing a present," Kilghannon said as he aimed at the locks on the door.

"It's coming!" Santos said under fire.

Kilghannon shot the lock off the door, the door smashed open, and there, face to face with him, stood a berserker.

"For once I'm glad to see your ugly mug, mate," Kilghannon said as he began to run.

The berserker crashed frantically as he screeched down the hallway.

"How close?" Kilghannon roared as he sprinted up the stairs.

"Ten seconds!" Santos reported.

Kilghannon ran through the roof access as the helicopter came into sight, now taking aim at the sprinting master corporal.

"Package delivery!" Kilghannon yelled as he quickly darted to the left, out of the way of the berserker, who now focused on the helicopter. The berserker roared as it jumped off the roof with great velocity, slamming into the helicopter and causing the pilot to lose control and begin spinning out of control.

"Kilghannon, you crazy bastard," Santos said.

"Don't tell anyone, but I forgot the RPG, had to improvise," Kilghannon joked as he regained his footing and joined the battle.

One helicopter hovered as men began jumping off it. The helicopter took aim and shot a missile at the northeast tower, killing both marines.

"Hostiles, northeast corner!" Smith roared as he helped Black up.

Malroy, now on his feet, looked groggily at the hell that had fallen upon this mission. A man ran across Malroy's sight in a chaotic fashion in the direction of the reported hostiles. Malroy then studied the man closer as he ran.

You son of the bitch, Malroy thought as he gave chase.

Malroy's body ached, and his head throbbed as he turned a corner down the pathway behind the mess hall and—just as he suspected— the man he was chasing came from around the corner.

Corporal Malroy speared him to the ground.

"Dr. Clase . . . I knew it." Malroy picked up Dr. Clase and slammed him against the wall. "What are you doing here?" Malroy demanded.

Dr. Clase struggled to get free, but Malroy punched him in the stomach, and then held him back up against the wall.

"Tell me!" Malroy demanded again.

"No, I think I'll let *him* explain," Dr. Clase laughed.

A Russian soldier punched Corporal Malroy in the face, causing his grip on Dr. Clase to slacken. Malroy stepped back and regained his focus. Dr. Clase watched on as the Russian soldier stepped toward Malroy. Malroy put up his finger, signaling to wait, flicking on his translator.

"I want you to know how much shit I am talking while I kick your ass," Corporal Malroy said as he raised his fist.

The Russian laughed and then quickly went for a left hook strike, but he was blocked and met with a counter right to the ribs, followed by a quick left gab to the face, knocking the Russian off his balance.

"I was always told Russians could fight—guess you are one of the exceptions to the rule, eh?" Malroy taunted as the Russian wiped blood from his nose.

"Leave Dr. Clase, go to chopper. I will handle this," the Russian instructed.

"Dr. Clase is in the base, east side heading to the hostile helicopters," Malroy reported.

The Russian yelled as he charged Malroy, blocking Malroy's left strike and slamming him against the wall. Malroy's body, already in pain from his jump, registered a sharp pain that tingled down his entire body as the Russian stepped back and cocked back his fist. Malroy grabbed his fist and quickly head butted the Russian as hard as he could. Malroy instantly regretted it, as he too felt immense pain in his forehead.

Dr. Clase had started to run when Malroy, as quick as he could, pulled out his sidearm and shot Dr. Clase in the left leg. Dr. Clase yelped in pain as he fell, clutching his now-bleeding leg. The Russian knocked the gun from Malroy's hand and punched him in the face, then grabbed Malroy by the throat, raising him off his feet.

"Talk shit now, little man," the Russian said.

Malroy struggled, trying to fight off the Russian

"Knife," Malroy managed to mutter before he kicked the Russian directly in the stomach, causing his grip to loosen. Malroy reached for the Russian's knife on his hip. Then, quickly snatching it from its sheath, drove the blade directly into the Russian's head.

Malroy, now sitting up against the wall, caught his breath as the Russian twitched once more before going completely limp.

"I have Dr. Clase," Malroy said as he looked over at the now-crying Dr. Clase. "Grow some balls, it's only a gunshot!"

***

Smith and Delmore continued to engage the Russians that had landed. Bullets pelted the now-destroyed barracks where Smith Delmore and Black had taken cover.

"Captain Petrov," Black said as he pointed.

Captain Petrov ran behind his line of men toward the nukes.

"He's mine, you to make sure the other nuke site is secure," Black said as he began to run toward the nukes, as well.

"Yes, sir!" Smith and Delmore roared as they fought on.

Petrov came up to the nuke control system and began punching in codes.

"Petrov to base, I have the nukes. Disable GPS grid lock- I have control now."

Black came up and tackled Petrov to the ground.

"You piece of shit!" Black spat as he slammed his fist into Petrov's face. Petrov lifted his hips slightly, causing Sergeant Major Black to become unbalanced, giving Petrov a chance to punch Sergeant Major Black off him. Both men regained their footing.

"Why?" Black asked.

"Motherland will be the supreme ruler," Petrov said.

"Why do you want the nukes?" Sergeant Major Black asked.

Petrov smirked as he charged Black, swinging quickly left and right; but these blows were dodged by Black, who was stepping back. Petrov stopped, and then went for a quick right hook, but his arm was grabbed by Black, who then turned and flipped Petrov over his back and slammed him to the ground.

Black went to grab Petrov by the neck, but Petrov in turn grabbed Black, pulling him closer and landing a head butt.

Petrov quickly reached for his sidearm and pulled it out, straightening his arm to fire, but Black pushed his hand toward the sky as a round fired off. Black gained control of Petrov's armed hand, trying to pry the firearm free. Black smashed his left knee into the rib cage of Petrov, and then landed another knee in the same place. Petrov's grip on the firearm loosened and it dropped to the ground.

***

Malroy got to his feet and slowly walked over to Dr. Clase, who was crawling in pain. Malroy kicked Dr. Clase in the ribs, and then pushed him onto his back.

"Why are you here?" Malroy asked.

Dr. Clase, clearly in pain, spat blood toward Malroy.

"Hey, you know there is an infection going around. Very unsanitary, Doctor," Malroy said sarcastically.

"I hope you burn in hell!" Dr. Clase said, enraged.

"Already here, buddy, now you better start talking, or you'll be getting round number two in the other leg," Malroy said, pulling out his sidearm painfully.

***

Sergeant Major Black and Petrov stood, facing each other eye to eye once again.

"Sokolov, get the other nukes ready!" Petrov ordered in Russian, but Sergeant Major Black's translator picked it up.

"Smith, stop Sokolov!" Black ordered.

Sokolov ran across the open gunfire and into what was left of the barracks; Smith quickly followed him into the building.

Four Russians remained as Delmore continued to fight.

"I need assistance here!" Delmore requested.

Kilghannon and Santos then stood up from the rooftop and fired from the air down upon the four Russians, killing two instantly.

Sokolov was almost at the nukes on the northwest side when he was tackled straight through a near-crumbled wall. Both Sokolov and Smith hit the ground hard as Smith quickly got on top and continued to punch the Russian. Left after left filled Sokolov's face, when suddenly, just as Smith was pulling his left fist back, Sokolov quickly smashed Smith in the face with a strong left. Both men got to their feet, but this time Sokolov tackled Smith down. Sokolov tried to mount Smith, but he was kicked off instantly and knocked through another near-crumbled wall. Smith got up and ran toward the Russian before he could get to his feet and rammed his right knee right into the right side of Sokolov's face, knocking him down again.

Smith caught his breath as Sokolov slowly got to his feet; Smith pulled out his 9 mm Browning pistol and pointed it at Sokolov.

"I'm taking you alive," Smith said as blood dripped from the left corner of his mouth. "We trusted you."

"We must finish what Dr. Clase started. Your country is too weak to realize what he can do!" Sokolov said. Then, with a smirk, "I am sorry, but we *won't* be taking you alive."

A Russian soldier came up behind Smith and stabbed him in the back, simultaneously pushing the gun away from Sokolov, and then stabbing Smith again, who now fell to one knee, gasping for air as it became harder.

The Russian soldier was about to stab Smith again, but Sokolov stopped him.

"Don't do him any favors," Sokolov said as they walked away

Smith, now lying on his back, was gasping for air. Thoughts of his wife and daughter flooded his mind; the smell of his wife started to invade his nose. The feeling of his daughter's hair between his fingers. A tear formed in his eye and began to fall down his face.

"Johnny . . . I'm down. Sokolov is heading for the nukes. Tell Linda I'm sorry," Smith said as he gasped for air.

Black heard his best friend over the radio, gasping for air and suffering in pain.

"Santos, get to Smith now!" Black roared as he fixed his sights back on Petrov.

Black charged Petrov with such rage, lifting Petrov off his feet and slamming him into the ground. Petrov quickly reversed and took control, kicking Sergeant Major Black off; both Petrov and Black got back on their feet. Black pulled his gun, but it was quickly swatted from his hand, followed by a right hook across the face.

Petrov pulled out his knife and went to stab Black, but was stopped. The knife edged closer to Black's stomach when he quickly turned and tossed Petrov up against a wall. Black now pulled out his knife.

"Come on, boy, you think I am scared of your little butter knife," Petrov said.

"You will be when it's embedded in your skull!" Black roared as he swiped at Petrov, who dodged it instantly and slashed Black's left arm. Black quickly pulled away, unfazed.

Black then went in again and missed Petrov, who then reached and stabbed Black in the rib cage. Black roared in pain as he stepped back and fell to one knee, holding his rib cage and bowing his head. His body ached, and pain shot through his entire body as it shook, barely holding itself up.

***

Santos reached Smith, who was lying on the ground as his breathing became slower.

"Brock!" Santos said as he slid down on his knee, holding Smith's head.

"Take . . . Take care of Linda and Rose," Smith said as his body shook. "Sokolov, nukes," he said, slowly pointing in the direction they had gone.

Santos knelt there, staring at a man he had known for ten-plus years. A man he had watched become a father, a husband, and one of his closest friends.

"It's okay, brother. They understand," Santos said gently as he held Smith's hand.

Smith's grip became looser and looser as his eyes began to shut.

"Rest easy, brother," Santos said as Smith's eyes closed and his hand dropped to the ground.

One tear fell down Santos' face and landed on Smith's face as Santos slowly put his head down.

"Sokolov!" Santos roared a deep, raged-filled roar as he ran toward the nukes.

***

Black heard his best friend's last words over the radio as Petrov stalked over to the injured Sergeant Major Black.

"You see, it was easy. We make you think we are your friend. You come into our control. You came to Russia, and didn't even know Dr. Clase was on your flight," Petrov laughed out loud. "You stupid, pea-minded Americans. It was a shame you wouldn't let Dr. Clase weaponize the cure. He could have made you great, but now Mother Russia will get to expand her borders to all of Asia. We will own half the world, and then maybe we take America." Petrov let out another laugh.

Black was now fading in and out as he became wobbly on his knee.

"Look at you, you Americans think you are so tough. The best part of it all, Sergeant Major Black . . . you die soon, so I tell you . . . you see this compound was actually a test sight. We found this compound, cleared it out, and gave it to Dr. Clase to finish his work. We supplied him human specimens and all his needs. We fabricate a story of a rogue general in a compound with nukes," Petrov laughed.

"Where do you think they got the nukes? We make China bow to his needs, rendering them handicap, not able to fight against us because we know China would never nuke their own people," Petrov continued. "Dr. Clase was so close to turning the virus on itself and making us an army of berserkers, and now with BlackNova soon to be dead, we will be able to complete his work." Petrov smiled. "Peace is for the weak, Sergeant Major Black. Just like your friend . . . He wanted to stop Sokolov . . . now he rots in hell," Petrov said, now standing over Black. Petrov put the bloody, cold blade up against Black's neck,

"Goodbye, brother," Petrov laughed, but he was cut very short as a steel blade ripped through the bottom of his mouth and into his brain.

"Goodbye," Black said with all his strength before falling down to his knees.

His side became warm as the blood continued to leak from the wound.

***

Meanwhile, Kilghannon and Delmore finished off the last two Russians as the gunfire stopped.

At the front gate, the fight raged on, infected continued to pour through the V-shaped front gate until it began to break. Running out of ammo, the Witter brothers pulled out their swords and braced as more and more infected strangled past the gunfire.

One infected ran up, but was quickly decapitated by Ryan. Another infected was stabbed by Rex, who was now beside his brother. A group of seven infected broke through the gate, and instead of running toward the gunfire, they ran toward the office.

"Ryan!" Rex exclaimed as he pointed.

"Marines, hold this position," Ryan said as he and his brother ran toward the group of seven.

141

Ryan whistled, which caught the attention of the infected.

"Hey, you lost?" Ryan said as he raised his sword.

The seven infected ran toward the two brothers. When the first one got close enough, Ryan swung the first stroke, dispatching the infected's head from its body. Rex came from behind Ryan and superman-stabbed an infected in the chest; his sword went so deep that he couldn't pull it out fast enough. Ryan quickly tossed his sword to Rex who, in turn, caught the sword, spun, and lopped off the head of another infected who was about to run past him.

Ryan ran and pulled the sword from the dead infected's body, and then ran toward Rex, who had just finished slashing one more infected down; Rex bent over as Ryan rolled over his brother's back and stabbed another infected straight through the right eye. He left the sword in the infected's eye. As it dropped, Rex tossed the sword to Ryan, who bent down and slashed another infected's legs from underneath it; as it crumbled to the ground, the last infected charged. Rex and Ryan stood together and simultaneously stabbed the last infected in the chest and then lifted it off the ground and ripped it into two pieces.

All seven infected dead, Ryan and Rex stood for a second and admired their work.

"King Arthur would have been proud to have us as knights of the round table, I think," Ryan said as Rex laughed.

***

Santos came around the corner and saw Sokolov and a Russian soldier standing near the nukes.

"Hey!" Santos roared.

Both men looked back as Santos raised his rifle and shot the Russian soldier dead in the head. Sokolov stepped away from the now-collapsed soldier.

Santos was now fixed on Sokolov.

"Do it," Sokolov said in his thick Russian accent.

Santos' hand quivered with rage as his finger grazed the trigger.

"No, Santos. We need one alive to prove all this was a setup," Black said as he stepped down slowly, holding his side.

"He left him," Santos said with pain in his voice. "He left him to die."

"I know, brother. But Brock wouldn't want this," Black said.

Sokolov then charged at Santos, who dropped his rifle and grabbed Sokolov, flipping him over his hip, grabbing his arm and snapping his forearm in half. Sokolov screeched in pain, holding his now-broken forearm.

Flames burned all around the compound; buildings lay in ruin as smoked billowed toward the warm night sky. One more gunshot was heard before, and for the first time, silence filled the air.

"Three men stay at the front gate, everyone else regroup in the middle of the compound. Kilghannon, please retrieve Smith's body," Black commanded.

Everyone converged in the middle of the compound. Malroy brought Dr. Clase over to the group and then tossed him into the middle. Everyone stared with rage as Santos joined the group and tossed Sokolov into the middle with Dr. Clase.

"Watchtowers, have an eye. More infected are surely to come," Black said as he returned his focus to the two men below his feet.

"Radio contact is down with home base—I'm not sure how we are going to get an extraction, gentlemen," Black said, looking around at his tired and battered men. Blood and dirt covered their faces.

All the men looked at each other as the possibility that they were going to die where they stood sunk in. Crackling fires surrounded the men as they all thought about the families they weren't going to see—the lips they would no longer kiss, the children they would no longer hold.

"Someone help me! My leg is bleeding still!" Dr. Clase demanded.

Malroy kicked Dr. Clase in the back. "You better get talking as to why this all went down."

"Sir, more infected approaching!" A marine warned.

A cold shiver went down Black's spine, but he could not show his fear—not now, not ever. He was a soldier. Black raised his head and looked at the men, nodding as he walked over to a flame and pulled out a metal piece of piping. Black them took the pipe and pushed it into his rib wound. Letting out a loud grunt of pain, he felt his flesh burning as he took the pipe away. Sergeant Major Black took a deep breath and picked up a rifle from one of the dead Russian soldiers, checked to see a full magazine, and reloaded it. Black turned back to his men and tossed the weapon to Ryan Witter.

"Gentlemen, we are the last line of defense. The nukes have been disarmed, and we stopped the so-called rogue general. But we now have innocent women and children in those living quarter huts. Once again, we are the last shred of hope for those civilians, and until the last member of BlackNova 8 has fallen, we will fight!" Black roared.

The spirit of the men surged as they were emboldened by the Sergeant Major's words.

"We fight for those who cannot fight for themselves, and we protect those who are fearful." Black roared to his men.

"Snipers in the towers, BlackNova 8 personnel, relinquish your ammo to those who need it and acquire your swords. BlackNova 8 to the front gate, marines to the towers. We hold this position," Black ordered.

"You, marine. Keep trying the radio, and watch these two. We need them alive," Black said. "Battle stations, men, and god be with all of you."

All the men raised their weapons and gave the loudest war cry of "Hoorah!" as they took their positions.

"Hello, this is BlackNova 8 and company, we are stranded in the compound located in Hailar, we require assistance urgently, does anyone copy. We have women and children. Does anyone copy," the marine pleaded.

Sergeant Major Black paused for a moment as he slowly pulled out his katana.

"Brother, if you are watching over us now. Give us your strength now," Black uttered to himself.

The groans and roars began to close in, and marines began picking off infected as they converged on the compound. BlackNova 8 stood strong in a line, facing the front gate.

"We hold this line! No infected gets through, men," Black roared.

Unified, the men answered, "Sir, yes, sir!"

"Don't stop fighting, brother," Rex said, looking to Ryan.

"Just try and keep up," Ryan answered sarcastically.

The first couple of infected breached the front gate and charged at BlackNova 8. Kilghannon stepped forward and slashed into one infected as Santos followed and finished off the second one.

Then, finally, the infected began filtering in through the front gate, roaring and screaming as they came face to face with their meals.

"Charge!" Black ordered as he raised his sword.

All the men shouted their loudest war cry as they followed their leader toward the jaws of death. Swords flashed, blood spurted, and war cries rang in the night. Two marines turned to the front gate and laid down fire, thinning the horde as it came through the front gate.

Ryan stabbed one infected in the head, then turned and slashed another across the face and punching another in the face. Santos sliced one infected across the waist, ultimately slicing it in half, and then stabbed another in the head. Kilghannon roared as he smashed his fist, which had acquired brass knuckles, into the face of an infected, then lopped off another infected's head. Delmore ran with his sword down and stabbed two infected together, but got his sword caught. Delmore then quickly pulled out his two side arms and began firing headshot after headshot into the crowd.

"Hello, this is BlackNova 8 and company, we are stranded in the compound located in Hailar, we require assistance urgently, does anyone copy. We have women and children. Does anyone copy," the marine repeated to himself again.

"We are all dead," Dr. Clase shouted. "Turn me loose, you fool, I can save the human race, and you are going to let me die!" Dr. Clase exclaimed.

"Hello, this is BlackNova 8 and company, we are stranded in the compound located in Hailar, we require assistance urgently, does anyone copy. We have women and children. Does anyone copy," the marine said again.

After a minute, the marine began to lose hope, his eyes closed as the realization began to settle in.

"Please . . . anyone. We need an extraction. We have many women and children," the marine pleaded.

Silence filled the radio waves as the marine collapsed to his knees with complete hopelessness.

"Copy that, we coming," a Chinese man answered.

"Hello? Hello? Can you hear me!" The marine jumped to his feet.

"We coming," the Chinese man said in broken English.

The marine jumped to his feet and ran outside, but before he could relay the message, an infected came from behind him and began ripping his neck out. His screams filled the ears of all his comrades.

One marine from the guard tower shot the infected in the head, and then shot the marine right after. The bloody battle raged on; fatigue began to overcome the adrenaline the men were feeling. It seemed the infected just kept coming, and that there would be no end in sight.

"Marines, out of the towers and focus fire on the front gate!" Black ordered.

All the marines turned their fire to inside the compound, which was becoming filled with infected. As hopelessness began to set in, and the men became almost too weak to wield their weapons, helicopters were heard in the distance.

Kilghannon cocked his head. "Santos, is that . . ."

"God, I hope so!" Santos answered as he cut down another infected.

Then, it was as if God showed himself that night. Bullets began to rain down on the infected. Missiles exploded outside the compound.

"BlackNova 8, on me!" Black roared.

All the men formed a circle as the helicopters cut through the infected.

"Chinese!" Delmore shouted.

"At this point, if they are hostile, I would rather die by a human hand then infected," Rex shouted as he stabbed another infected.

Two helicopters broke off and tossed down four rope ladders as they began to hover.

"The women and children!" Santos shouted.

"Rex, Ryan, go!" Sergeant Major Black ordered.

The brothers sprinted toward the living quarters. They burst into the rooms.

"Run to the rope ladders!" All the women picked up their children and began running out of the huts.

Chinese soldiers slid down the ropes and formed a circle.

"Behind, behind!" a Chinese commanding soldier ordered.

BlackNova 8 pulled back behind the line of Chinese soldiers who were picking off infected left, right, and center.

"Up, up!" the Chinese commander ordered.

"Women and children first!" Black answered as he pulled out his sidearm and shot two infected that were charging him from his left side.

Women and children came from around the corner led by Rex, who began helping them up the ladders.

"All you got men, we aren't out of the woods yet!" Black roared as he slashed an infected in half.

The Chinese soldiers and BlackNova 8 formed a circle around the ladders, allowing the women and children up first. Infected now covered the outside of the compound, and the tree line disappeared within the horde of infected.

"Kilghannon, go up with Smith's body now!" Black roared.

Kilghannon sheathed his sword and ran over to Smith's now-cold body.

"You are coming home, brother," Kilghannon said as he picked up Smith's body.

Malroy looked over and finally noticed the dead marine that was supposed to be watching Dr. Clase and Sokolov.

"Shit!" Malroy yelled as he ran toward the office.

Malroy ran in and saw Dr. Clase half out the door, limping.

"Come back here!" Malroy yelled as he gave chase to Dr. Clase.

Dr. Clase was now outside limping down the pathway behind the workshops. Malroy came out of the building and closed in on Dr. Clase, but just before he got a hand on Dr. Clase, Sokolov slammed into Malroy, knocking him down.

"Die!" Sokolov yelled as he raised his pistol and pointed it at Malroy.

A gunshot filled the air; Sokolov slowly collapsed to his knees and a stream of blood began exiting his head and running down his face. Malroy looked over and saw a Chinese soldier standing as he pointed his rifle at Dr. Clase.

"No!" Malroy yelled. "We need him."

The Chinese soldier nodded and walked over punching Dr. Clase in the stomach then began to tie his hands.

Hey, tying his hands . . . that's not a bad trick, thought Malroy.

"Back to helicopter," the Chinese soldier ordered.

Malroy, now holding Dr. Clase as the Chinese soldier killed infected, moved toward the helicopter.

***

Everyone else was now aboard the helicopters, and they laid deadly cover fire down as Malroy and Dr. Clase began to climb the ladders. The Chinese soldier killed a few more infected and then jumped on the ladder. The helicopter began to take flight away from the compound.

Santos looked down at the compound, which was now fully infiltrated by infected. Like ants on an anthill, nothing but infected swarmed the compound.

"Thank you," Santos said slowly to a Chinese soldier.

All of BlackNova 8, for the first time, took a breath. They rested their heads against the backs of the seats as the helicopter took them far away from the hell they had just lived. Black looked over the body of his now-deceased friend.

"I failed you, brother," Black said as he rested his hand on Smith's chest.

The helicopter ride to Qiqihar in Heilongjiang province was quiet. All the men now had time to mull over the fact that they had lost a brother. Everyone had their own memories playing in their heads that whole ride home. Black was dreading the phone call he would have to soon make to Comox 19 Wing to tell Brock's wife, Linda, that her husband was not coming home to her and their daughter.

Despite surviving against all odds, the flight was somber. It was always that way when a comrade was lost; most men feel it should have been them. Survivor's guilt burns for a long time. Smoldering questions would linger. *Why and how did I survive? What did I do right that gave me another day? How do I best honor the memory of my fallen comrade?* Also, the ride home was filled with aches and pains now that their adrenaline had worn off and their bodies began assessing the ordeals they'd been through.

A Chinese woman looked over at Sergeant Major Black who was clearly in deep thought, and gently touched his hand.

"Thank you," she said in very broken English.

Sergeant Major Black, at that moment, was not touched by the woman's kindness, for his heart was nowhere to be found. At first, he had lost his wife and daughter, which devastated him, crushed him, and left him, if anything, an empty shell of a man.

Through everything, Smith had been there for him—through the toughest of days, and the okay days. Major John Black came to the realization that he no longer had anything or anyone to live for.

15. CLEANUP

QIQIHAR, CHINA
JUNE 19, 2024 (03:00 HOURS)

The helicopters landed at the Chinese base in Qiqihar and were met by medics and base personnel who helped everyone off and examined everyone for the virus before admitting them to the rest of the base.

The doctors looked at everyone's eyes for red blood vessels, as this was an indication of infection. BlackNova 8 got off the helicopter and waited nearby. A doctor came up to Sergeant Major Black and inspected his knife wound that had been cauterized.

"You do this?" the doctor asked.

"It's fine, flesh wound," Black said.

The base commander was a colonel by the name of Zhang Fei. He walked up to Black.

"We radio your base, you can talk then," Fei said in better English than expected.

"Thank you," Black responded.

Malroy was standing near the helicopter as Dr. Clase's leg was finally being attended to.

"Don't treat him too good," he said. "Where he is going, he will wish he were dead."

"Please leave your weapons here and follow me to the radio room," Colonel Fei said.

All the men dropped their weapons and followed the Chinese commander. They walked into a room with big TV screens and people running around wearing headsets.

"That room, please," Colonel Fei pointed.

All the men walked into the room as the colonel shut the door.

"Hello?" The voice was that of President Frank Gallagher.

"Mr. President?" said Black.

"Oh, thank god," the President said as people in the back could be heard cheering. "We lost contact with you men once the GPS was shut down. I'm not sure what happened, but I'm sure glad you are all okay."

"Not *all*, sir," Sergeant Major Black said softly.

"Oh, dear, I am sorry, gentlemen. We will speak soon, no time to mull over everything yet. We had a Globemaster dispatched as soon as China gave word they picked you men up. Last check the pilots were still about a day away, refueling in Germany. I hope to speak to you all soon."

"Sir, it was a setup!" Ryan Witter shouted.

"Excuse me?" Gallagher said.

"Russia was behind the whole thing, sir," Black explained.

"I'm lost, what happened?" the President asked.

"Jiang Maiyong was a cover. If he ever existed, he's probably long dead. We were told a rogue general wanted to nuke all of Asia, but in reality, the compound belonged to Dr. Clase and the Russians. They knew we would intervene when nuclear war was threatened. They sent us into the compound to get slaughtered, but it would just look like a failed mission with no survivors. We have reason to believe that Russia wants to claim all of Asia, sir," Black finished.

"Sir, Master Corporal Santos here. I was in the office building and saw maps of targets they were planning on nuking from China, which we all know would make China public enemy number one, and Russia would look like they were trying to stop China. The Russians crippled China by demanding food and water, and if China said no, they would nuke all of Asia from the compound in China," Santos finished.

"Gentlemen, these allegations are serious," the President said.

"We have Dr. Clase in custody, sir. I personally killed Captain Petrov as he tried to kill me, but before I killed him, he told me they had someone in America hide Dr. Clase on the Globemaster during our first trip to Moscow, and when we arrived there, they got him off without anyone knowing. I was in the medical wing when we returned, but everyone reported that they were put into the barracks and were escorted everywhere; now we know why: so we would not see Dr. Clase working," Black explained.

The President was silent for a moment.

"President Volkov had his own agenda, sir. He was never about peace," Delmore added.

"Find out all you can from that scum Clase," the President demanded. "And come home, gentlemen, we have much to discuss." The President signed off.

In the White House situation room, the President was furious. He muttered something under his breath.

"Sir?" General Summers said.

"I didn't even see it—he played me. I thought we had a new world of peace," Gallagher said, now physically shaken with rage.

"We will sort everything out, sir," General Summers assured the President. "You can count on that."

***

Back in China, Sergeant Major Black walked out of the communication room and saw a high-ranking Chinese official standing with some soldiers. They locked eyes for a moment, and then the official motioned Black back into the room. Black followed his orders and walked back in, followed by him.

"Everyone leave but him," the Chinese official ordered.

Everyone looked at Sergeant Major Black with worry in their eyes; they were unarmed in China, knowing they had previous combat history.

"We prefer to stay together," Malroy inserted.

"It's okay, gentlemen," Black ordered.

All the men left the room and were escorted to a room three doors down.

"Sergeant Major Black, my name is Young Kim, I was the one that ultimately ordered the rescue."

"Then I thank you for that," Black said. "None of us would have made it out otherwise."

"Sergeant Major Black, I want you to understand that we did not know about the Chinese citizens being held hostage at that compound. We were under the impression it was merely another rogue tribe just trying to survive. Once I heard your radio call to protect the women and children, I jumped to action. Your actions were honorable; regardless of previous events, Sergeant Major Black, you put Chinese lives before your own, and we respect and honor that. We mean no threat here."

"Well that's good news, but you can understand my distrust at the moment given we were just attacked by infected and Russia at the same time," Sergeant Major Black explained.

"You will be delivered home safe and untouched. President Sung also sends his thanks for protecting Chinese lives. There are political items to work out between our two nations, but above all, you saved Chinese lives, disregarding your own safety. The President admires you and your team for their moral code.

"We appreciate that, thank you. I don't mean to be rude, but where is my friend's body?" Sergeant Major Black asked.

"Your friend has been off loaded and is in the resting room, until your flight arrives. We can escort you. We did not want to offend, so we have set up an area for mourning," Kim said.

Black now stood before Kim, taken aback by Chinese generosity, humbleness, and devotion to their citizenry.

"Thank you, for everything. Without your help, none of us would have made it out of there," Sergeant Major Black said.

"Please, let me take you to your friend now," Kim said.

***

Everyone stopped at the door and allowed Johnny his moment with Sergeant Smith, who lay peacefully with his arms at his side in a makeshift coffin. Johnny approached the coffin and looked down Brock's face. He stood in silence, staring at his lifeless friend.

"I'm so sorry, brother," he said as his emotions overcame him. "It should have been me, you have a family. You had so much left, and I let you down."

His body shook with rage and sadness, and he felt like his final lighthouse in life had gone dark. Sergeant Brock Smith had been the one to get Major Johnny Black through everything he had suffered.

Andy Santos and Seth Malroy came up behind Johnny Black and rested their hands on his shoulders. As they stood over the body of Brock Smith, they could be human and show weakness for once.

16. HOMEWARD BOUND

The next morning came slowly as all the members of BlackNova 8 laid sleepless, thinking about their fallen comrade. All the men were ready and waiting the next morning as they were told the Globemaster was inbound in ten minutes.

They waited in the loading area, gear and weapons in a pile with two Chinese soldiers guarding it.

"When will you make the call?" Santos asked Black.

"When we get home. I'm not sure how to tell Linda," Black said as he looked away from Santos.

"You'll find the words, brother," Santos said as he dropped the topic.

The Globemaster came into view and began its decent to the runway. It was a warm day that day. The air quality in China was a bit worse than in the USA; the men found it was almost like a thick smog that hung over them all day. The Globemaster came to a stop and the men began approaching the plane.

As the men loaded, the Chinese President came onto the runway with his guard. Sergeant Major Black turned and saw the President come toward him.

"Sir," Sergeant Major Black said saluting, showing respect.

"Thank you. I wanted to personally say thank you for saving our citizens. From what I am told, you gave the order to protect them. You showed great discipline and courage. I look forward to the phone call I will have with your President," President Sung said, extending his hand.

"Our pleasure, sir. Citizens first, always," Sergeant Major Black finished.

"Always," President Sung smiled as he began to walk away.

"Safe travels," Commander Brian said, extending his hand.

"Thank you again for the assistance," Sergeant Major Black said, extending his hand.

Commander Brian nodded to Black's appreciation and began to follow the President.

Malroy and Santos carried Sergeant's Smith makeshift coffin into the Globemaster. Delmore and the Witter brothers grabbed most of the gear and loaded it into the place. Their old dirty clothes from the mission reflected the hell they had just been through.

"All aboard, sir," Kilghannon roared.

Johnny took one last look around as the heat pressed against his face. "Rest in peace, brother. We will meet again," Johnny said, walking up the ramp as it began to close behind him.

CPSIA information can be obtained
at www.ICGtesting.com
Printed in the USA
LVHW03*1459060618
579811LV00004B/55/P